Love & Bravery

sixteen stories

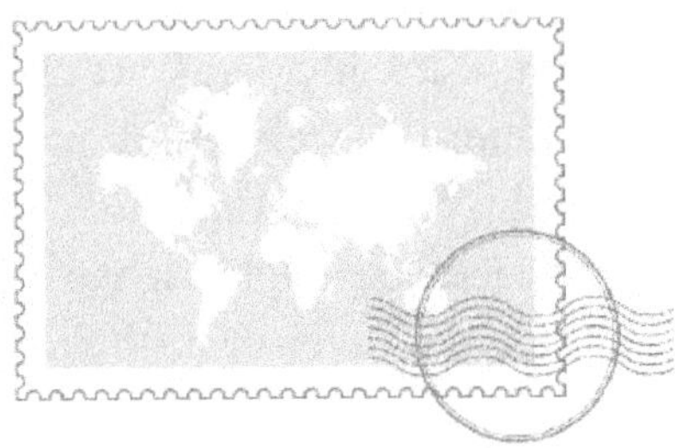

Suanne Laqueur

Suanne Laqueur/Cathedral Rock Press
Somers, New York
www.suannelaqueurwrites.com

Publisher's Note: This is a work of fiction. Names, characters, places, and incidents are a product of the author's imagination. Locales and public names are sometimes used for atmospheric purposes. Any resemblance to actual people, living or dead, or to businesses, companies, events, institutions, or locales is completely coincidental.

This book depicts situations involving consenting adults having consensual adult sex using adult language. Reader discretion advised. Batteries not included.

Love & Bravery/ Suanne Laqueur. – 1st ed.
ISBN: 978-1-7345518-6-0

Introduction

I write one of two ways: gargantuan, epic novels spanning decades and generations with multiple themes and intricately-woven plots. Or I write little isolated moments in time, capturing the middle of the action without worrying much where things started or where they'll end up.

This little book is the latter. A collection of love bites, if you will. Most of these can't be called stories because they lack a proper arc. Some are anonymous, some are named. They all touch on the notion of bravery. Because love is always worth the risk.

Enjoy with courage.

–SLQR
December 22, 2017
Somers, New York

LOVE
&
BRAVERY

THE NEXT LIFE

Lovina Beach, Bali
Indonesia

They hadn't given the room two glances when they arrived. The door barely clicked shut when she put down her bag and hurled herself at him, threw her arms up tight around his neck and found his mouth with hers. He stumbled back, opened his hands, let keys and wallet and whatever else he was holding drop to the floor. He picked her up, whirled her in his arms. Once. Twice. Then he threw her down on the bed.

"Ever been fucked by a retired man?" he said, pulling off his shirt.

"No," she said. "I hear it's life-changing."

They tore each other apart nine ways to Sunday. Erotic madness, all night long. They made love to sleep and woke to make love again. Over and over until they were exhausted, spent and sprawled across the mattress in a tangle of arms and legs. She vaguely remembered crawling to the bathroom at some point in the pre-dawn hours, then to the mini-bar, coming back to bed with a bottle of water which they both gulped at like patients suffering from fever. Then they sorted out the covers and careened back into sleep.

Now, in the full light of morning, she opened her eyes and looked beyond the square footage of the mattress. To her surprise, she found her gaze level with the horizon. Her side of the bed faced the large, curtain-less picture window. Last night it had been an inky block on the wall. Now it framed the ocean, side to side. One endless expanse of indigo, a crystalline black line where it met the pale blue sky.

She pushed up on her elbow. Now a swathe of bone-white sand filled the picture. She slid noiselessly out of bed and stood at the window, transfixed by the view. Blue ocean, dappled with white, as far as her eyes could see. The horizon curving ever so slightly at the edge of her periphery. Not a trace of humanity was visible. Not a soul, not a footprint. Only endless waves lapping the shoreline and a pair of seagulls hopping in the shallows.

"You're beautiful."

She looked back over her shoulder. He lay on his side, watching her, just his head and one shoulder out of the covers. For several minutes neither of them spoke or even smiled. They stared, connecting over the small space between them, finally taking in what this morning meant.

Slowly one of his arms emerged from beneath the comforter, unfolded across the expanse of mattress where she had been a minute ago. His fingers reached to her. Something so tender and yearning about how they uncurled and stretched into the air, wanting her.

"Come back," he whispered.

Holding his gaze, she came and put her hand in his, let herself be drawn down. He pulled her against his chest, ran his hands over her head and kissed her face, then gently rolled her so he could hold her from behind.

Tucked in his arms, small and sheltered, facing the window and the view, she snuggled her shoulder blades into his chest. Feeling him hard and impatient against the backs of her legs, as he was so often hard for her in the mornings.

So many mornings of quick fast love in the hours of dawn. Only a few moments to linger tenderly afterward, before he had to spring from bed and put on his game face, go back to that other world where he belonged.

He'd risked everything to start the business. He'd risked his youth and his relationships and his health to build it and keep it and maintain it. Now he'd risked everything to leave it.

"Otherwise, what was it all for?" he said.

Still, retiring young took guts. Selling the farm, downsizing and hitting the road was the new American dream, but you had to be brave to take the first step.

All the little acts of courage led them to today. Now the ocean and sky lay spread out before them, the day stretched into a glorious vista of nothing to do and nowhere to be. The world, at last, was theirs.

He, at last, was all hers.

"Welcome to the next life," she said softly, tilting her hips back and guiding him inside her.

A low sigh of contentment rumbled deep in his chest. His arms wound tighter about her body. He crushed her against him and buried his face in her hair. "I didn't think it would ever happen."

Her hands slid along his forearms, wrapped around his wrists, held onto him. "You feel so good."

He pushed into her further, pulling her deeper into his lap. His mouth was so soft on her neck. "This is all I want today," he said. "This. Only this. Just having you whenever I want."

"We'll just stay in bed all day?"

"All day," he said. "I mean it."

"Do you?"

"This is what I've waited for. Just to ignore time, throw it away. I never want to wear a watch again."

She laughed softly in his embrace, his happiness splashing onto her, his delight so tangible as he went on.

"I'm never going to ask you what time it is. Ever. The only time I care about is when we're going to make love next."

She freed one hand and reached it back over her shoulder, caressing his face, feeling his smile in her palm, running her fingers through his hair. "You'll have to feed me at some point."

"Oh I'll feed you all right." He gathered up her hair, moved it aside and set his mouth at her nape. "You'll need the energy to keep up with me." He was moving more intently now, moving with a purpose, holding her where he wanted, sliding into her quick and sure and hard.

"Oh really," she said, trying to sound blithe but he was moving in her. He had nothing to do but be in her, so hard, so hot, and she was starting to come apart.

"You have no idea," he said, kissing his way carefully down her spine, a little bit of teeth on her skin, a little touch of his tongue on her bones. "I'm gonna fuck you until you can't remember your name."

"I'd like to see you try," she whispered, the words falling apart in her mouth because he was in her and it was coming on. Coming around, rising up over her like a rogue wave. Always in the mornings when his body was coiled tight with insistent longing but hers was still wreathed in sleep, he could make her come so hard and so easy, even if they didn't have much time. But now they had nothing but time and she could have him any way she wanted—fast, slow, hard, gentle, tender, filthy, they could make love or they could carelessly screw, or any variation in between, all day, all night. Nothing but time and nothing but him and she needed nothing else, not even her own name, which was gone now, it was his name in her throat, in her chest. His name she called out to the morning, his name in the ocean outside the window and the life they had waited for stretched out beyond the horizon.

Bois Bandé

JALOUSIE PLANTATION
SUGAR BEACH, SOUFRIÈRE
SAINT LUCIA

ROGER WENT FOR A WALK around the grounds after dinner, hoping to find his lost sunglasses, finally running them to earth in one of the cabanas. Triumphant at avoiding the hassle of getting a new pair, he strode through the open-air lounge and saw their waiter, Guillaume. He was at the bar, off duty, having a drink. Gui waved him over enthusiastically, urged him to sit.

"Drink with me. You have time, or Miss Stavi wait for you?"

"She's at the spa." Roger pulled up a stool and sat down.

"How about an Irish Moss?" Gui said with a grin.

Roger groaned. Their first night in the restaurant, at Gui's urging, he'd tried a shot of that vile seaweed extract and one was enough. The memory alone made him gag.

Gui laughed, clapping him on the shoulder. He summoned the bartender. "Simon. A Piton for my friend."

A draft of the famed St. Lucia ale was pulled and set

on a coaster before Roger. Gui was having something strange and dark in a lowball, at the bottom of which lurked a single chili pepper. Simon had fixed himself the same.

Apparently Roger had been invited to witness a transaction of some sort, for after the men clinked glasses and drank, Simon dug in his shirt pocket and produced a small plastic bag of brown powder which he slid across the bar. Gui made an exclamation of delight, picked up the bag and showed it to Roger.

"Bois bandé," he said.

Roger looked at him blankly.

"Gui has a new girlfriend," Simon smiled. "That shit there, hé? Make you love like a tiger."

"Ah." Roger tried to sound knowing.

Gui was holding out the bag, clearly wanting him to inspect it. Roger took it, and tried to look appreciatively at its contents, although it could've been cocoa powder for all he knew. His brain helpfully piped up with some scrap of useless trivia. He looked over at his companions and ventured a guess. "Rhinoceros horn?"

Simon rolled his eyes and replenished his drink with another chili pepper.

"That's a Chinese myth," Gui said. He had taken back the bag and was delicately opening it. "This? The real thing. Better than ecstasy. And no headache tomorrow. You try?"

"What is it? I mean, what's it made of?"

"Richeria tree," Simon said. "Native to Caribbean.

You peel the bark and the inside, you grind it down."

"Sometimes they steep the whole bark in rum," Gui added.

Simon grew stern, raised a warning finger. "Not as good. It's weak, see, the bark, it does not dissolve."

"It's fine for tourists," Gui said.

Simon set his finger at his temple solemnly. "You steep the whole bark in rum, you need seven rum to get the effect. Tiger won't find a lover on seven rum, hé? But just the inside bark, ground like this, is fine. Strong. You only need a little and the tiger finds you."

Once more Gui held out the bag and Roger stared, intrigued, but out of his element. Was he supposed to take a pinch and snort it? Eat it? Unzip his fly and sprinkle therein? He considered, debated the wisdom of taking candy from strangers, and then finally said, "I will if you will."

Apparently this was exactly the right thing to say for a simple, yet serious ritual followed. With the panache of the practiced bartender, Simon laid out a small rattan mat, three fresh lowballs, and began setting up bottles and ingredients.

"First, rum," he said, doing a high pour into a clean shaker. "This from British Virgin Islands. The best. A name like that, you can't go wrong, hé?"

He turned the label toward Roger, who laughed when he read Pusser's Rum.

Simon was in the zone now, a high priest at the altar. A vanilla bean was split and scraped, the seeds delicately tapped into the rum. A lemon was muddled with a small piece of fresh ginger and the juice strained into the shaker. Another jar came up from under the bar.

"Some add molasses to this drink," Gui said, "but Simon use Nevis honey. From the Nisbet Plantation."

"Liquid gold," Simon said softly, "the tropical flowers give it a taste. You find it nowhere else but Nevis."

Expertly he let a ribbon dribble into the concoction, turning the jar to cut off the stream without wasting a drop. He capped the shaker, took an end in each of his large hands and gently tilted it this way and that.

"Gentle," he said, smiling. "You treat this drink like a woman."

"Stir. Don't shake," Roger said, fascinated by the ceremony and enjoying himself immensely.

Cap off with a flourish, and into the waiting lowballs Simon poured a beautiful amber shot, his keen eye portioning precisely. He then pushed the glasses together to form a triangle and produced a small spoon. He dipped into the bois bandé and dropped a dose into Gui's shot. Gui took the spoon and administered Roger's drink. Roger doctored Simon's. They gently whirled their glasses in circles on the table until the powder dissolved, raised, clinked, and downed.

"Wow," Roger said. "That's fantastic."

And it was. Smooth as silk, the citrus, the ginger, and the vanilla masking the bite of the dark rum, and the honey a pleasant aftertaste.

Like a woman, Roger thought. He tilted the glass to

get the last drops. "What do you call this again?"

"Bois bandé."

"That's the name of the powder, or the name of the drink?"

"Both."

He waited for his head to explode, or something as dramatic, but nothing happened. Perhaps a delayed reaction. He hoped he wasn't going to completely trip out at the bar. As he chatted amiably with his new comrades, he monitored himself closely. Was he sweating? Breathing hard? Becoming paranoid? Other than feeling warmly buzzed from slamming a shot of 95 proof rum, nothing else seemed to be happening mentally, nor was he suddenly sporting wood or consumed with lust. Maybe, like the rhinoceros horn, it was all a myth.

He shrugged it off. What difference would it make anyway? Since arriving at the plantation, scarcely an hour went by when he wasn't itching to get his hands on Stav. They were on a veritable roll of magnificent sex: on the beach their first evening, twice yesterday, again this morning. He didn't need any help, thanks much, but what the hell, too late now.

He went to pay but Simon waved his money aside, shook hands instead. "The tiger find you," he said gravely.

Roger dismissed that as well. He didn't know from tigers.

"Tell lovely Miss Stavi good night," Gui said, shaking

hands. "See you in the morning."

Roger left the bar feeling nothing more than a general, suffused contentment. But some time later, in the dark of their room, lovely Miss Stavi lifted her face out of the mattress with a concerted effort and pushed her tangled hair out of her mouth. Her shoulder blades were heaving and slick with sweat.

"Oh my God," she said, gasping. "What is *with* you tonight?"

"Bois bandé," Roger said.

"The hell is that?" A luxuriant groan as she lay her head back down. "Jesus, I can't see straight."

His beautiful orange-and-black paw stroked her back. "You all right?" His voice was a honey-coated, rum-soaked purr in his ears.

"Oh, I'm fine..."

SILLY RABBIT

A Train from Paris to Milan

They met in Paris.

This is not to say they met for the first time in Paris, for they had met years before at the University of Delaware. He was a sophomore and she was a first-year grad student. The affair shot like a meteor across the red-bricked campus. They made out beneath the Kissing Arches which, according to legend, meant they were destined to marry. But in the end, he was too young and she was too driven by ambition. The meteor fell screaming to earth, leaving a bigger crater in his heart than he liked to admit. A depression he filled with booze, weed and unsuitable girlfriends until his parents threatened to pull the plug on paying his tuition. Then he filled the void with words, writing articles for the UD Review and penning a secret sloppy novel on weekends. His English professor gave him an intro to an agent and there must have been good bones in the slop because he had a book deal before he had a degree.

He walked into his first meeting with his publishing team and there she was. Again. Twenty-six now, a junior editor. Gorgeous. And married.

He was involved himself, the hole in his heart's landscape filled, graded and planted with flowers. So a pleasant year passed, peppered with laughing lunches, ripshit literary arguments and a smoldering low-key flirtation made all the more sweeter by the lack of intention. He went on a signing tour and when he called back in at the publishing offices, she was gone. Divorced and done wrong, she'd fled for Europe.

When his own relationship fell apart, he wrote to her at a forwarding address he was sure was expired. It wasn't. They began a correspondence. He sent postcards, she wrote on sheets of translucent air-mail stationery. Innuendo wove around the words and between the lines, the flirtation bold within the safety net of distance.

Then one day, she called.

"What are you doing?" she said without preamble. The satellite connection roared in the background like the ocean separating them, and he was surprised at his lack of surprise. He supposed he'd been waiting for this.

"Right now?" he said, yawning.

"Between right now and the next month or so."

"Writing."

"I have a proposition for you."

"Well, it's about time." He turned off his computer and took the phone over to the couch.

"Are you dating anyone?"

"No. How about dinner?"

"How about Paris?"

"What's in Paris?"

"Me. Also L'Hôtel des Deux Continents."

"And what are you doing there?"

"Waiting for you."

Her casual audacity didn't surprise him either. He lay back in the couch cushions, enveloped in a thrumming happiness both excited and dismissive. "Sure," he said. "Be right there."

"Don't you want to see me?"

"Silly rabbit," he said.

"We'll take the train to Italy."

"That's not fair."

"I'll pay."

He sat up now. "You're serious about this."

An exasperated sigh. "Do we need to start over?"

"Is that what we're doing?"

The silence swelled until he wondered if the call had dropped.

"I've been thinking about you," she said. "And I'd like to see you."

"In Paris."

"Yes."

The next day, an overnight envelope arrived, containing a ticket on Air France from Kennedy to Charles de Gaulle. And a note:

Meet me Gare de Lyon, Wednesday, 8:30 pm (Paris time). Train departs 8:56. I'll be wearing a hat and carrying flowers. For love prior to departure, meet me same place as soon as you arrive. I'll wait all day.

"You're crazy," he said, tapping the ticket against his teeth. "You are out of your mind." Whether he was addressing her audacity or his actual consideration of the idea, he had yet to determine. His heart was thumping the same way it would thump when her envelopes would arrive in the mail.

Needing a voice of reason, and a second opinion, he called his wisest friend, Bill.

"Scenario," he said.

"Shoot," said Bill.

"Your ex-girlfriend from college calls last night. I mean ex-girlfriend with a capital G, the one you kick yourself for letting get away and marry some creep. Now she's divorced and she's in Paris and she wants you to come visit. This morning a plane ticket comes to your office."

"And?"

"No 'and.' That's the whole scenario."

"You writing on a deadline?"

"Yeah."

"Can you write from anywhere?"

"Yeah."

Bill chuckled. "And you need *help* with this?"

"No, it's just..."

"Dude. This is the moment your future self will kick you for not seizing. Be brave."

He found his courage and his passport, packed a bag

and his laptop and abandoned ship.

Wednesday morning, not dawn, but early enough, the taxi dropped him off at Gare de Lyon and she was waiting for him, sitting prettily in a shoeshine chair, chatting up the attendant. She wore a straw fedora with a feather in the band, and across her lap was a sheaf of red roses. She threw them to one side and the hat to the other, jumped out of the chair and into in his arms.

"Waiting long?" he asked, holding her tight.

"Years," she said, sighing.

He put his face in her neck, pushed her hair aside to get at her skin, and inhaled the past. "It's the same perfume," he said.

"Bought it 'specially," she whispered. "What do you want to do first?"

He kissed her.

"Coffee, croissants and love?" she asked.

"Not in that order."

And they got back into the taxi. "St. Germaine-des-Pres," she told the driver. "Rue Jacob, vingt-cinq."

* * * * *

HE WAS JETLAGGED. She was patient. In her small room at L'Hotel des deux Continents, they lay naked together. Not making love yet, just exchanging long caressing strokes with the flat of their palms. No urgency as she caressed and kissed him. No clear intentions. They were simply here and getting acquainted again.

It was Heaven to touch, to trace her curves and recall her scent and count her freckles and remember the slide of her skin and bones under his palm. Countless times he was sure he was falling asleep, but sleep never quite came. He lay blissfully unhinged, lucidly dreaming. Fingers laced behind his head, he smiled into the dimness while under her hands, his erection came and went like the tide.

He drifted in and out, in varying degrees of desire. He wanted to come but didn't know if he had the energy to take her. The edges of his mind began to dissolve. She was saying something, but he couldn't discern if she was really there or just a dream he was touching himself to.

He opened his eyes fully, shook the clouds from his head. She was here and he was hard, full of blood and intent. He was in Paris and it was her hand on him, not his.

The floodgates opened and lust came pouring forth in a torrent. Before he could roll onto her, she climbed on top of him, enfolding his head between her forearms and the curve of her throat, enfolding his cock into her warm, magical wetness. Then she had him. Her body moved, grasped and released him like a glove, fucking just the tip of him and then impaling herself down to the base, over and over, bringing him to the brink then drawing him back. Her hands held his wrists pinned when he tried to grab for her waist. Her legs held him down when he tried to buck his hips up underneath her.

She was a strong woman and he fought her. But after

a few writhing trips to the brink and back he surrendered. He lay beneath her, doing what she told him to do, saying what she told him to say. Through it all she murmured that it was for him, all of it, anytime he wanted, as much as he wanted, all of it for him.

She fucked him into near-insanity. He ached. He pleaded. He groaned. And when he came, he came forever, his eardrums bulging against the morning.

When the tremors of his body subsided, she rolled off him and he followed, taking her into his weak arms and kissing her. When he leaned and closed his mouth around one of her nipples, she took his other hand, pushing it down and guiding his fingers. He took up the rhythm she set and kept up until she came. Sleep was quick to follow, and twilight found them with arms and legs tangled together like wild grapevines.

He awoke first, and turned immediately to her body, stroking her back and hair until a short sigh from her throat indicated she was at least conscious, if not completely awake.

Sleepily, eyes still closed, he stroked her body, the curves of her breasts, the long flat plains of her belly and leg muscles. The sharp ridges of her ribcage and hipbones. The crinkly softness of her pubic hair. Cautiously he probed the cleft between her thighs, warm and sticky from love. At that, she shifted and lazily reached to take him in her hand, making him hard with a few caresses.

"Do we have time?" she murmured, finally opening

her eyes and glancing toward the clock.

"We always have time," he replied, pushing into her heat, although it was actually late and their train would be leaving. His sweet, stubborn silly rabbit. There was plenty of time.

Still, they barely made their train.

* * * * *

THEY HAD A SLEEPING COMPARTMENT on the Napoli Express, which would arrive at Rome's Stazione Termini at 2:30 Thursday morning, but they planned to get off at Milan first. They were starving. When the train stopped in Mulhouse, outside the Swiss border, platform vendors were pacing the length of the train, selling picnic boxes. He leaned out the window to buy while she clutched him from behind, counting francs and translating.

They had no table, no silverware and no glasses, so they sat on the floor and opened their treasure box. They ate with their fingers and drank red wine out of the bottle. They ate until their lips shone with olive oil, and the kisses they exchanged were redolent of basil and oregano and cinnamon pastry.

Outside the window, Switzerland was moonlight and mountains. He sat on the bench seat with his feet propped on their bags while she fed him the rest of the olives, letting him suck the oil off her fingers. Hooking an arm around her neck, he pulled her mouth into his, ran his other hand down her leg and then up her skirt.

They'd run out of the hotel so fast, that she wore nothing under the black georgette. *In the altogether*, as his grandmother would say.

He was just as bare as she beneath his pants, and she freed him without pushing them down. Crawled astride him and put him inside, letting her body rock and fall with the train's clackety-clack rhythm. She rolled off his lap, guiltily, when the conductor knocked and came in to let down the beds. It took him five minutes to set the berths and wish them bonne nuit.

As soon as the door clicked shut, he had her up against it. He hit the light and the cabin plunged into darkness, illuminated with regular bursts of light from outside the compartment window. Each strobe light flash across her face imprinted her on his mind, a series of snapshots catching her in the throes. This moment. Now this one. This one. This.

They collapsed in the drafty berths with their paper pillows and thin blankets. The compartment was so narrow that they could reach across the space between their bunks and grab hands, but they didn't do this until morning, when the sun was coming up over Lombardy and the conductor was knocking again, bringing bread and coffee.

SACANAGEM

THEY WEREN'T DOING WELL.

Emerging from their hotel door was not so much stepping into the street as it was being swept up into a mosh pit. They had no control over where they were going, they simply had to follow where the current led them. It took an hour to move three blocks, inch by humid inch. The air was oppressive, the crowds defied description, and the flower his lover had tucked behind her ear was beginning to wilt.

So was she.

This, plus the heat and the noise and the uncertainty of how to get back to the hotel, was making him decidedly edgy. They needed to sit down somewhere but so far all they had managed to do was wrench themselves from the riptide, press their backs against a brick wall and stay out of the way of the sweaty, sexed-up throngs that comprised this bloco of Salvador during Carnavale.

It was simply beyond everything: innumerable people drinking, shouting, dancing, kissing. In an uncontrolled explosion of happiness that flung sexual shrapnel over 700 meters of streets. It seemed the perfect recipe for a riot, yet no menace was in the air. Not the slightest edge of danger as strangers greeted and groped. The world was genuinely and unabashedly in love, lust hung in thick clouds and the skies rained permission for anything and everything. It was exhilarating, overwhelming...

And if only they could sit down for two damn minutes and take it in.

Then, salvation: a young couple sitting at a table at one of the cafes that lined the street, waving at them. Them? The couple nodded, pointed, made beckoning gestures, pointed to two empty chairs.

Come! Sit!

He grabbed her hand, and without breaking eye contact with these two wonderful stranger-Samaritans, muscled his way through and across.

The couple introduced themselves as Eduardo and Rafaela. They were both painfully beautiful and extraordinarily friendly. He spoke English, she did not, but she clucked and cooed over them in Portuguese with concern that needed no translation, and she summoned the waiter as if by imperial decree, ordering well-iced drinks. Now, from the safety of their ringside seats, finally hydrated, basking in Rafaela's tactile hospitality, the American couple relaxed into the atmosphere.

"First time at Carnavale?" Eduardo asked.

The foreigners nodded absently, looking in all directions, taking in the dancing, the music, the breakdown of social order, the air of possibility that pervaded everything.

"Dentro de quatro paredes," Rafaela said, touching both their hands, "sob os lençóis, e por trás da máscara de carnaval, tudo pode acontecer." She sat back with a knowing air. They all looked at Eduardo to translate.

"Within four walls, beneath the sheets, and behind the mask of carnaval, everything can happen," he said.

"Tudo," Rafaela repeated with satisfaction. She spoke again, at length, and Eduardo again translated.

"Brazilians tend to allow expressions of sexuality and eroticism that are quite unacceptable in other areas of the Latino world," he said. "Especially in public. 'Everything,' or tudo, refers to the world of erotic experiences and pleasure. The phrase fazendo tudo, 'doing everything,' means Brazilian men and women have an obligation to experience and enjoy every form of sexual pleasure and excitement, or more precisely, those practices that the public world most strictly prohibits. This, however, must all be done in private, between four walls, under the sheets, or..." Here Eduardo gestured expansively, indicating the swirl of revelry around them, and said, "Behind the mask of Carnavale."

"Sacanagem," Rafaela said, and her voice dripped a dark, luscious secret. Eduardo half rolled his eyes and muttered something dismissive. She swatted his arm and spoke her mind.

"It doesn't translate well, sacanagem." He smiled at

the Americans, his hand warding off Rafaela's gentle beating as his brow wrinkled in thought. "It means...the world of erotic experience," he said. "Or perhaps the erotic universe. It doesn't matter. Tudo and fazendo tudo are key elements of sacanagem. A Brazilian most clearly embodies the erotic ideal of sacanagem by doing everything, particularly that which the public world condemns and prohibits. The transgression of public norms brings the playfulness of Carnavale into everyday life."

The Americans nodded, a little bewildered by this lesson in a cultural concept alien to them. Now Eduardo and Rafaela were having a heated debate. Or rather, heated on her end, and Eduardo responded with a tender tolerance.

Lost in the sparring Portuguese, the American woman drank the last of her beer and looked over at her lover, tousled in his loose, white shirt, his fingers slowly rubbing his chin, regarding their hosts with fascinated amusement. She took in the tilt of his head, how the streetlights turned his skin golden and caught the blue in his eyes. She ran her fingertips along his forearm, from wrist to elbow, up under his sleeve. She thought about his body under his clothes and a longing ache settled down low in her lap.

He felt the heat in her touch and looked at her. His heart splashed in his chest. She had her ballerina on, poised and delicate in her white dress with her dark hair drawn back. He reached and took away the crumpled blossom in her hair, smoothed the damp tresses behind her ear, ran his fingers along her jaw. He drained the last of his beer, then he lay his hand, cold and wet from the bottle, on her leg under the table, pushing up her skirt to get his palm full of her smooth skin.

His mouth watered. His eyes narrowed. He moved his hand further up her thigh. She uncrossed her knees, sat back a little in her chair, raised her chin at him and let her own gaze soften and blur.

They stared. Seconds stretched out like taffy. A hole opened in the night, and they began to creep toward its rim. His cool fingertips reached the lace edge of her underwear and deftly slid beneath. The table, the street, their Brazilian friends, all receded, grew faint, dim. She slowly pulled her knees further apart. She was wet and easy and his fingers inched up and into her. His chin rested on his other hand, elbow on the table, expression innocuous save for his eyes—his eyes smoldered as his fingers slid in and out of her, glossy and warm.

Sacanagem, she thought. She was going to come. He was getting her off. At the table. In public. In front of strangers. He had never done such a thing. But the way he was looking at her, intent, unsmiling, not teasing, not letting up on her...

"Go on," he whispered, low enough for only her to hear. "Go on..."

She tilted her hips, rocked down on his hand, breathing softly through her mouth, not looking away. Her face didn't betray the slightest thing until the tiniest of orgasms made her close her eyes for an instant of piercing pleasure. She opened them again, stared at him, fell into him. Her fingernails bit down into the skin of his arm. She called to him, but no sound came forth.

He held his hand still then, awed by the shape of her mouth around his name, feeling the pulse of her around his fingers, the hot wet core of her, that crux of everything she was. He stared. He thought he had never seen her look so beautiful...

An audible clink broke the spell. Eduardo had set his beer bottle down on the table, and set his other hand gently on Rafaela's mouth. She stopped talking, and Eduardo leaned forward to them on his elbows with eyes that missed nothing.

"Basically all this is to say my wife is trying to get you in bed," he said.

"Me?" they both answered at the same time, and Eduardo threw back his head in a magnificent roar of laughter. "Yes, you. Both of you. Look, take advantage of the fact that she doesn't have a word of English, finish your drinks and go back to your hotel."

She sat forward and he discreetly withdrew his hand from her skirt. They both shut their mouths and exchanged tentative, American glances. Eduardo laughed again. "Hesitation," he said. "Bravo. I like that you at least consider the offer. But trust me, amigos, this isn't what you want. You only want each other. Go back to your hotel and fazendo tudo."

He asked where they were staying and scribbled a

small map on a cocktail napkin. He stilled any last protestations Rafaela had, and she capitulated with kisses on their cheeks and a heady rush of perfume.

Eduardo embraced his American mate heartily, fists thumping his back. "Your wife is beautiful," he murmured. "I saw you making her come under the table."

"She's not my wife."

Eduardo laughed once more. "Fazendo tudo, trás da máscara de carnavale."

As quickly as they had been rescued from the crowd, the Americans were jettisoned back into it. Armed with directions and heads spinning with fervent, feverish thoughts, they made their way through the bloco and were swallowed up. Gone.

At the table, Eduardo watched them disappear, then he kissed Rafaela. "Sacanagem," he said. "I never think it's going to work but fuck damn, it gets them every time."

She preened in his embrace with the air of one who knows she is always right. "That was stupid easy. How long was that, what, all of twenty minutes? One drink each. Child's play."

"I liked them."

"You liked her, you mean."

"Oh, as if you weren't eating him alive with your eyes, he's totally your type."

"Ai meu Deus, did you feel the heat coming off them?"

"Did you feel the moves under the table?"

"When he kept whispering *go on...* I almost came myself. And her face the whole time? She barely blinked. She's good."

They kissed a little more, teasing and giggling. "They have to be back in their room now," she said.

"Either that or he couldn't wait and he's got her up against the wall in an alley."

"Oh please, there isn't an unoccupied alley in all of Bahia tonight."

They both howled with laughter, slapping the table. "Definitely their room," she gasped, wiping her eyes. "What do you think they're doing?"

"Fucking like gods," he answered. "What are they not doing, is the question."

"He's definitely finishing what he started," she said. "He can make her come like that under the table in a crowd, think what he can do alone in the dark."

"She's coming, Rafé. Right now. As we speak. She's under him, a beautiful mess, crying out his name. Can you see it?"

"She was lovely." Her eyes blinked sensuously as she ran her hand up his thigh and into his lap. "You're hard for her. Right now."

He crossed one knee over, trapping her hand, drank the rest of his beer, and neither confirmed nor denied.

"I can't believe you let them get away." Her hand in his lap was expert.

"It was better."

"We could've had them," she said, insistent.

"No," he said. "No, he wouldn't share her."

Then Rafaela nudged him and indicated with her head across the street. He looked, flicked his eyes back to her and nodded. Her hand withdrew from his lap. They put on their masks: big smiles and expressions of concern. They waved at their new catch. They beckoned grandly. They pointed to the empty chairs.

Come! Sit!

Blind

I MET MY WIFE on a blind date in January of 1996, during the winter semester of my senior year. I was majoring in Special Education at Virginia Wesleyan, with a concentration in teaching techniques for the blind and deaf. I was required to do a year's internship in both fields, and I had spent the fall term as an assistant teacher at the American Sign Language Institute in Manhattan. Second semester found me at the Lavelle School for the Blind in the Bronx, a twenty-minute commute by subway from my tiny apartment on the Upper East Side.

The blind date was arranged by a mutual friend and, as I later found out, looked forward to with mutual dread. I'd been single for the year and a half since calling it quits with my longtime girlfriend, whom I'd dated since eleventh grade. All the miscellaneous, unsuccessful dating I'd endured had me fill out the *Marital Status* box on forms with "Out there," or "Transitional."

Socially speaking, I found Manhattan a cruel anachronism. For all the hustle and bustle of seven million people occupying one little island, connection was in short supply. The signature energy of the city was made up of countless individual force fields. Every commuter crammed into a bus, subway or other public space had an inviolate privacy shield constructed around them. A spark ignited whenever two shields brushed, and all those overlapping, bumping, brushing edges within the shared space created a current of Together Alone that drove production forward and moved day into night.

I stepped up my southern pace to New York's stricter tempos. I curbed my ingrained habit of saying good morning to everyone I encountered, and learned how to make my eye contact reach the boundary of my privacy shield but go no further. I struggled with loneliness. I'd never felt it before. I missed my friends—the childhood pals still kept close and the newer, complex circles of buddies from college. I didn't know how to meet new people in Manhattan. Lavelle didn't provide me with an atmosphere that would lead to after-hours socializing. The majority of the faculty at the school was older, most married with children. With the few that were closer to my age I did make superficial, work-related liaisons, but nothing that materialized past the three o'clock bell. I joined a gym, formed a few casual acquaintances who included me in pick-up basketball or squash. Every now and then I crossed paths with alumni from VW passing through for the weekend, but nothing ever panned out past Sunday.

As for meeting women, forget it. It seemed the only

opportunities I had to meet them were in bars or the grocery store, and if you think you stand a chance of meeting the love of your life at the corner pub or in the frozen food section, you live in Disneyland.

It was a cold winter that year. To say it was a social dry spell and an all-out sexual draught conjures images of a desert. Instead of a Bedouin on a camel, I felt like an Antarctic research scientist lumbering along in a Sno-Cat, waiting for the sun to peek over the horizon again.

Mary Catherine Streany, whose class I was assisting, innocently asked if I was dating anyone, and I responded with a detailed commentary of the pickings at hand. The evenings of polite yet pallid chemistry. Life stories over drinks. Forced conversation and weak laughs over dinner. The litany of "this was fun, I'll call you," with no intention of calling.

"Guess you're not getting any lovin'," Mary said.

"Good guess," I muttered.

Looking back now, I can't imagine why any woman in her right mind would have wanted to spend ten minutes in my miserable, cynical company. And I don't know what divine force was at work when my de facto boss regarded my sorry ass and put two and two together.

"Maybe it's the girls you're asking out," she said.

"You know any better ones?" I said over my cup of instant oatmeal. I was always a little surly before I'd digested breakfast.

"I think I do." Her expression was mysterious as she

flipped open the cover of her bottomless Rolodex and walked her fingers through the cards.

"Wait, you're fixing me up? Don't." I tried to reach for the one she pulled out but she slapped my fingers away and dialed the phone. I tried to depress the hang-up button and got slapped again. A veteran mother's Cut The Shit slap.

"Nina Valenti, please. Mary Streany." Tucking the phone securely into her shoulder, Mary reached into her bottom drawer where she kept her cookie stash. She gave me a Fig Newton.

"Please hang up," I said. I hated Fig Newtons.

"Be brave, Mack," she said in a dark whisper. "Nina? It's Aunt Macy, how are you, darling?"

Aunt Macy? I mouthed. Setting me up with her niece, was she out of her mind?

"I'm fine, fine, Hank's on the road and the boys are crazy, business as usual. Yes. Listen, cookie, forgive me being a yenta, but there's someone I want you to meet. Oh, don't be ridiculous, you don't have to marry him, just go meet him. Be brave. If you don't like him then maybe he's got a friend..."

At that point I left the room with my oatmeal and my detested Fig Newton and let Mary do her dirty work in private.

Fine, I'd have a blind date with the niece. But it wouldn't be incongruous with my luck if I did go out with this girl and she ended up marrying one of my buddies.

* * * * *

MARY WAS SWEETLY OBNOXIOUS about keeping the date as blind as possible. I managed to yank out the information that her niece worked part-time at Bloomingdales while building up her clientele as a massage therapist. Mary refused to divulge any physical description, so I was forced to create my own image of Nina Valenti. I pictured an overly made-up cosmetics clerk working her way through beauty school. Or a soft, lank-haired, granny-dress and crystal-wearing hippie who never shaved, wore fur nor touched meat.

Groping for an optimistic attitude, I decided that if it didn't work out as a date, at least I'd have a massage therapist's card in my wallet.

So there I was, standing outside Carmine's at Broadway and 44th Street on a Thursday night, preparing. Which meant I was second-guessing the tie I had worn, grimacing over the zit that had appeared on my chin, and formulating a plausible excuse in case I had to make a quick getaway. A prayer was also in order:

Please God, let this one be different. Let her be intelligent and funny and clear-minded and able to hold up her end of the conversation. And if she can't be all that, then at least let her be gorgeous. Or easy. Or both. Thy will be done. But if it goes badly, don't let her run back to Mary with any embarrassing details. Don't let me be the subject of Thanksgiving conversations. While you're at it, I'd like a million dollars. Thank you. Amen.

Stepping out of a cold winter night and into Carmine's was like being hugged by a garlic-roasted grandmother. It was a family-style restaurant with phenomenal food and Old Country ambiance that even I, with my phosphorescent Irish hide, could appreciate. Nina and I were to meet at the bar at seven. It was only quarter of, so I checked my coat, grabbed a stool and ordered a beer.

Scoping down the length of the bar, I ticked off six men in business suits and three couples. At the far end, a lone woman in a purple sweater was working the crossword puzzle and drinking a Bud Long Neck. The kind of woman who made you wish your blind date wouldn't show up.

Oh my, said something inside. *Oh my eye. Yes indeed.*

I took short, quick glances at her, synchronizing them with short, quick sips from my beer. I drank in her cascade of long, red curls. Not a colleen's strawberry-blonde, but deep, rich Crayola colors: auburn, brown, mahogany, chestnut, burnt sienna. Dangerous hair. The kind you want to drown in. One look and you're tangled in it like a web, wanting to plunge your hands wrist-deep in it, feel it on your back, your chest, behind your knees.

She seemed oblivious to the lethal weapon on her head. No fussing with it, flipping it from one shoulder to the other, gathering a handful away from her face and letting it slide through her fingers. No constant rearranging. I watched her for ten straight minutes and she never touched it.

Oh my eye...

I tore my gaze away before I started drooling. I checked my watch, finished my beer and ordered another. At five after seven I started getting antsy. By ten after I was annoyed. I was always on time for dates and women were always late. Fashionably late. Bullshit, it was a way to build suspense, make an entrance and subliminally gain the upper hand. The whole business made me want to—

"You Al McKenzie?"

The bartender was talking to me.

"Me?"

"Yeah, you. Al?"

"Yes."

"You're keeping your date waiting."

"I am?"

"You are." Grinning from beneath a thick mustache, he flicked his chin toward the far end of the bar. "Down there. The redhead with the Bud Long Neck."

I looked.

She raised her eyebrows, mouthed "Al?"

"Holy shit," I said.

Al McKenzie, c'mmawn dowwwn!

"Hurry up, man," the bartender said. "Before I ask her out myself."

I tumbled off the barstool and walked on invisible legs down the length of the bar.

She was blushing. "Hi, I'm Nina."

I was sweating. "Hi, I feel like an idiot."

"So do I."

"How did you finally figure out I was me?"

"Well, I was waiting and you looked like you were waiting so I took a shot."

"Good shot."

"You obviously didn't think I was me."

"Well, I was hoping it was you, but..."

Her eyebrows raised. "But?"

"I didn't think I... I mean, I'm not usually so lucky."

She gave me a long sideways glance over her beer. A skeptical smirk twitched at her mouth, which then widened into a pleased smile. "Sit down, you."

"Yes, ma'am." I clambered up onto the stool beside her. The bartender brought the beer I'd left at the other end of the bar and set it before me, shaking his head and chuckling.

"We made his night," Nina said. "Thanksgiving, generations to come, he'll be telling the story of the blind date that almost wasn't."

Thank you, God, I thought. *I'd love to be the subject of that Thanksgiving conversation. Thank you. You're so wise. I was a fool to doubt you.*

"So you're a massage therapist," I said.

"Yes I am."

"And you also work at Bloomingdales."

"I see Mary gave you the rundown."

"A little of this, little of that. I can't imagine what she told you about me."

"You want to know?"

"No."

She leaned on an elbow. "You're from Virginia, you want to be a teacher of blind and deaf children and you're Generation X's answer to Robert Redford."

Mary said *that?*

"I guess two out of three ain't bad," I said.

"You're not from Virginia?"

I slugged her lightly on the upper arm. "Sit down, you."

She took a prim sip of her beer.

"So, are you one of those women at Bloomies whose job it is to spray perfume at everyone?"

"God, no. I work upstairs in corporate."

"Doing what?"

"Marketing research. Data analysis. I help decide which perfume gets sprayed."

"Oh."

"Obviously it's not what I went to school for. It's a temporary gig but the money's good. It pays the rent. I've been trying to build up my clientele since I got my license."

"License?"

"In massage therapy. You have to be licensed to practice."

"Do you just have private clients?"

"A few, and I have hours at a spa in the village. That's my evening job."

"So you work days at Bloomies, nights at the spa...

What do you do on weekends?"

"I work at a strip club called Flashdancers."

Our eyes held and I felt the edges of our Manhattan force fields give way and overlap. "You're either the girl of my dreams or the one my mother warned me about."

"Your table's ready, Miss," the hostess said behind us.

As we studied the menus and chatted, I learned Nina grew up in Westchester County, north of the city. She'd graduated from Fredonia State with a degree in Sports Medicine, and she'd been living on the Upper East Side for two years.

"My parents own the apartment," she said. "I don't think I could swing it otherwise. Don't get me wrong, I pay rent. But as far as Manhattan rates go, it's a steal."

When the waiter arrived, she shocked me by speaking to him in fluent Italian.

"Do you know what you want?" she asked. "Or can I order for us?"

"Go ahead," I said, happy to follow where she led.

"Anything you don't eat?" Her gaze deepened and our overlapping edges melded together, filling my stomach with a different kind of hunger.

"I'll eat anything," I said.

Including you.

In all my dining out years, I'd never been ordered for. This meal was a blind date within the blind date and I dug not knowing what was coming next. Which was unlike me.

We had soup, an antipasto platter and Caesar salad

to start. Then rigatoni with sausage and broccoli. I could've gone back to Carmine's the next night, ordered the exact same things and not in a million years would they have tasted so good. Something about good company enhances food like nothing else, and Nina's was the most delicious presence I'd ever been at table with.

We talked easily, exchanging the usual gamut of first-date information: job descriptions, school days, encapsulated life stories. Interwoven in the small talk was an easy familiarity. Plates passed gracefully back and forth. We tore bread, passed butter and licked our fingers. She leaned on her forearms and I mirrored her. I leaned back and she did, too. I was so comfortable, I filched a black olive right out of her salad with my fingers—a habit my ex-girlfriend detested. Nina only shrugged and pushed the plate further toward my side of the table. "Take them all, I hate olives."

We killed two bottles of wine and staggered outside around nine thirty. The cold night like a slap in the face. Winter bounces off all the steel and concrete in Manhattan and invades your bones. Especially in January, when the holiday decorations have been taken down and you have no festive joy or anticipation to warm you.

"I forgot gloves," Nina said, buttoning her coat up to her chin.

I gave her my gloves and stuffed my hands in my pockets. Our elbows bumped as we walked into the snow whipping down Broadway. We talked carefully, aiming our words away from each other—Carmine's food is laden with garlic.

"Well, I had a good time," I said, as we neared the 49th Street subway entrance.

"Me, too."

"I had a great time, actually."

"Me, too." She smiled at me. Her cheeks were pink and snowflakes stuck on her eyelashes.

We sat side-by-side, first on the N/R train to 59th Street, then on the 6 train uptown. My arm and hip pressed up against her arm and hip. One combined bubble of wine-and-garlic privacy.

"Can I see you again?" I asked as the train pulled into the 68th Street station, the stop right before mine. "I'd really like to see you again."

"Yes." She fumbled in her purse and brought out a pen, stuck it between her teeth while she fumbled around some more and dug out her business card. She motioned for me to turn away, then leaned on my back to write down her home phone. Her hand rested, warm and flat, on my left shoulder blade. She put the pen away and I looked at the card:

Nina Valenti.
Licensed Massage Therapist.
Swedish. Shiatsu. Reflexology.
By appointment at Oasis Day Spa.

The doors exploded open at 77th Street. My future wife put out a hand and squeezed my arm as I got up, then waved through the window as the train pulled out again. I stared down the tunnel until the tail lights disappeared. I dropped a dollar into the open guitar case of a street musician playing Elton John's "Daniel." I walked home, calculating moments, minutes and hours until I could see her again, debating an acceptable interval to wait before calling her. And of course, lusting for the feel of her hair in my hands.

Nearing my apartment building, it occurred to me she hadn't given back my gloves, nor had I asked for them. I relished the idea of something of mine going home with her. Touching her skin by proxy.

I was happy right then. The New York cold in my bones silvery with promise. For the first time, it felt like *my* city. My home. I'd finally cracked the code and figured this place out.

I met someone.

Instead of coffee, I would bring Mary Catherine flowers in the morning.

At quarter after eleven, I was lying on the couch in fleece sweats and wool socks, flipping channels. My phone rang and when I answered, a woman's voice asked: "What's a four-letter word for 'stupefy?'"

I blinked at the walls. "I'm sorry, what?"

"What's a four-letter word for 'stupefy'?"

"Who is this?" I said, stupefied.

A click of tongue against teeth. "What do you mean,

who is this?”

I sat up. “It’s you,” I said. Actually, I yelled it.

“How quickly they forget,” Nina said.

“Holy shit.”

“Surprised?”

“Frankly, yes.”

“Well, I figured the only way to keep from waiting for you to call would be to call first.”

“Clever. Clever. Exactly what I would’ve done.”

“So why didn’t you?”

“Because I said I’d call. I can’t say ‘I’ll call you’ and then call, it’s against all the rules. Do you know what kind of trouble I’d get into with the American Male Society?”

“Huh. So what’s a four-letter word for ‘stupefy?’”

“What crossword are you doing?”

“The *Times.*”

“Hold please.” I reached for my messenger bag and wrestled out the *Times*, struggling to open and fold back the sections while keeping the phone clamped to my ear. “How far along are you?”

“I just started.”

“Good. Race you?”

“Race?”

“Last one done buys lunch tomorrow.”

“I can’t wait until lunch. Loser buys breakfast.”

“Where?”

“Coffee shop near me. Second Avenue and 78th Street.”

“You’re on. Call when you’re done. Go.”

"…"

"…"

"You didn't go," she said, laughing.

"Neither did you."

"Okay, I'm going."

"Okay."

"Okay?"

"Okay." She laughed again. "Jesus."

She hung up. I tossed aside the paper, leapt up and ran for the closet. I dug her business card out of my overcoat pocket and dialed.

"I lose," I said. "I buy breakfast."

"Who is this?"

YOUR NAME

Saint John, New Brunswick
Canada

She's wearing an avocado-green coat today. She can get away with unusual colors.

I don't know her name. I've never said a word to her. Not *hello* or *good morning* or even *excuse me*. She's just a woman I've been watching for two months.

Every morning around eight-twenty, when I am in the Lighthouse Deli getting my coffee, I see her getting off the ferry from Nova Scotia. She comes into the Lighthouse and gets coffee, then walks up Chalfont Street to catch the bus.

I catch the same bus. She gets off at University Avenue, across from the UNB campus. I get off one stop later, on Sandy Point Road. This business is all reversed in the evenings, except for the coffee. She goes straight to the Ferry. I go home to my apartment.

My bedroom window faces Saint John Harbor. As I loosen my tie at the end of a day, I look out the window and I can see the ferry. I can see her, too, if it's a clear day and if she's wearing something distinguishing and stands on the outside starboard deck.

I take off my work clothes while the boat glides past Negrotown Point, growing small and fainter. I put on jeans or sweats and watch until the ferry slips past Partridge Island and becomes nothing but a smudge of smoke on the horizon.

On the bus in the mornings, I watch her. She tears out a mouth-shaped tab in the top of her coffee-cup lid. She drinks in tiny, scalding sips and chews patterns of teeth prints into the Styrofoam. Does she take her coffee black, I wonder. Light no sugar. Light with a lot of sugar.

She's a little thing. I've never gotten close enough to measure, but I imagine she'd come to below my shoulder. Her black hair is cut a little past her jaw, parted off center. One side falls in waves, the other she habitually tucks behind her ear. I don't know what color eyes she has.

She doesn't have a ring on her left fourth finger. I was quick to notice one crowded day on the bus when she was standing in the aisle, her ungloved left hand grasping one of the uprights. She wears a silver ring on her right thumb. Sometimes she wears glasses. Sometimes when the evening bus stops at University Avenue, she's standing in the shelter smoking a cigarette. Once she got on with a tissue paper cone of roses in her arms. Another night she boarded with a half-pound bag of Doritos and ate them the whole way home, with one ankle crossed over the other knee and a newspaper in her lap. She was working the crossword puzzle.

Tonight, she just sits and picks at her nails. She smiles at some people. She talks to no one. She doesn't see me.

I make up names for her. She looks like a Maria. Or maybe a Maggie. Perhaps something unusual and exotic, Zoë, Naomi, Isabel. Or something more classic, like Katherine. Patricia. Christine.

I want to blurt out to her, "What's your name?"

I want to peek in her shoulder bag for some sort of clue. I wish she'd drop something on the street or leave something behind on the bus.

I'm thinking of stealing her scarf.

Lisa. Mary. Nancy. Kirby. Stephanie. Nicole.

I walk to the gym, work out and wonder her name. I walk home talking to her inside my head. If the block is empty, I'll talk out loud.

"I see you every day," I say to storefront windows or a lamp post. "My name's Tim."

I clear my throat shyly. "Hi, I'm Tim, how are you? What's your name?"

I hip open my apartment door and toss down my backpack in exasperation. "You know," I say, laughing. "I *see* you every day. I'm *madly* in love with you. Who *are* you?"

I think of the V her hair makes at the nape of her neck. I imagine her head would fit perfectly into my curved hands. I hold them out in front of me, at the level I estimate her head would come to. I close my eyes and kiss her red-lipsticked mouth.

What does her skin smell like? What would be the

texture of her black curls on my fingers? How old is she?

Alison. Robyn. Jenny.

Jesse?

Samantha. Susan.

I go running down by the wharves, panting in the smell of fish and algae and the oily, metallic stench of the ferry engine. Across the bay, Nova Scotia is cool and pine-green, smudged by a misty curtain. She's over there somewhere. The ferry docks in Digby, but perhaps she lives in Clementsport or Clementsvale. Deep Brook. Bear River. Lequille.

I could ferry over, taking my bike along. I could ride around looking for her. But that's ridiculous and stalkerish and I'm not brave enough yet.

Laura. Michelle. Debra. Celia. Becky.

* * * * *

"BREAKFAST OF CHAMPIONS."

These are the first words she ever speaks to me.

It's another ordinary morning. We've gotten our coffee at the Lighthouse Deli and now we're boarding the bus. She's wearing a hat today. A slouchy black velvet one with the brim flipped up in front and fastened with a taffeta rose.

She looks lovely. I don't think I've ever used that word so readily before. She's lovely. She's *charming*, dammit.

We sit opposite on the bus. If we both straightened

our legs, our feet would touch in the middle of the aisle. She takes a few sips of coffee before wedging the cup between her knees. The flower on her hat bobs slightly as she digs around in her shoulder bag and pulls out a bag of candy. Carefully opens one end and then she's munching peanut M & Ms at seven o'clock in the morning.

I think I'm in love.

I'm transfixed, utterly unable to tear my eyes away. When she turns her head and her gaze snags on mine, I'm filled with panic but I can't look away.

What's your name what's your name what's your name...

And then she smiles.

She shrugs a little and her chin dips toward the yellow bag of candy. "Breakfast of champions," she says.

To me.

She says it to me.

I smile. My mind is an abyss of complete nothingness. My face frozen in a grin until she breaks the connection and looks away, as matter-of-factly as one would hang up the telephone.

My mind springs to life. Breakfast of champions. We now have a private joke. I take the ball and run, plots and plans whirring off my brain like sparks from a grindstone. I'll start bringing her a bag of M & Ms in the mornings. Starting tomorrow. I'll just toss it casually to her, and say, "Here, brought you breakfast."

No, wait, I'll sneak a bag into her pocketbook and let

her find it and wonder.

No, no, wait, I got it, tomorrow I'll bring her a bagel with cream cheese and say, "Your breakfast habits are starting to worry me."

Maybe I'll wait and see if she has M & Ms again tomorrow. If she doesn't, I can say, "Hey, no breakfast today?"

I plan and reject. Plan and reject. In the end, I am so full of ideas and anticipation that I simply cancel myself out like an equation, come full circle back to where I started, and the next day, I do nothing.

I get coffee as usual. She doesn't come into the Lighthouse Deli. Disappointment stirs in me like winds before a storm, gently ominous. They grow into gusts as I walk up Chalfont Street, glancing over my shoulder toward the pier, trying to pick her avocado-green coat out of the crowd. I step up and onto the bus and flip my pass at the driver. He slams the doors on my day with a vacuum suck of hissing air. She's not here. The ferry has docked, the bus is leaving, and she's not here.

It's never occurred to me she might not come one day.

Gloomily I ride along, moping over my coffee. I wonder if she's sick. Did she have a dentist appointment? Maybe there was an emergency in her family. Maybe her car broke down, or she had to bring it in for servicing. Maybe she overslept and decided what the hell, she'd stay in bed and take a day off.

Perhaps she has a lover staying in bed with her, too.

The day goes rotten.

I sulk about my classes and watch the clock. I'm short and curt with students and I snap at the department secretary, then have to go back and apologize.

At night I board the bus with the hope she was merely running late this morning and took a later bus. But we stop at University Avenue and she doesn't board. The rest of the ride seems to take twice as long. Funny. When she's there, the ride can't be long enough. Without her, it can't be over too soon.

I just want the ride and the day to be over.

This void in my insides created by her absence worries me. Who is she to me anyway?

Who is she?

I miss her.

Maybe I should be brave and tell her.

* * * * *

THE NEXT DAY, she's at the Lighthouse, standing last in line. She smiles when I step up behind her.

"Morning," she says.

Her hair's wet at the edges. She's not wearing any makeup and looks incredibly tired.

"How are you?" I say, my voice raspy, which I've been told on occasion is rather sexy, so I refrain from clearing my throat although it's starting to itch really bad.

"Tired," she says.

"Yeah, me, too." I'm not tired at all, actually. I fell

asleep on the couch while reading last night. Eight and a half hours of prime Z's.

It's her turn to order. Lou, the counterman, gives her a big hello and asks, "The usual?" and she nods.

He gives her black coffee. "Anything else?"

Her curls swish back and forth as she hands over some change.

"Have a good day, chèrie." Lou turns his face to me, then. "Yes, sir, Mr. McKenzie, regular coffee, right?"

I nod, preserving my voice. I watch her dump two sugars into her cup and wonder if she's heard my name. She stirs, replaces the lid, crumples up her wrappers and drops them in the basket by the door. The bells on the jamb jingle. She's heading up Chalfont Street.

I was hoping she'd wait for me.

I hope she heard my name.

* * * * *

"HOW WAS YOUR WEEK?" she asks as we step off the bus.

"Uneventful." *(Except I got to watch you put on your makeup while we rode in on Monday. Tuesday you smiled at me. Wednesday you said you liked my tie. Thursday you made the bus driver wait while I came tearing up the street, out of breath and late and wearing two different shoes. And now it's Friday and you're talking to me.)* "How was yours?"

"Same old same old."

"Such exciting lives we lead."

"I can't stand it."

"Are you a student?"

"Mm." She stops at the kiosk on the corner of Place des Ravins and looks over the bunches of flowers. "I'm doing an internship. I'll only be around here until May."

I wonder if she's trying to tell me something by that.

She picks a cone of bright orange roses. "C'est combien?" she asks the vendor, a burly man sitting on a pile of magazines and smoking a pipe.

"Pour vous? Cinq."

She gives him a dazzling smile I've never seen before. The idea to pay for the flowers myself blooms in my mind but she hands over the money before I can act on it. We continue down Chalfont Street.

"I like that color," I say, taking the cone of paper from her and peering in. "I've never seen orange roses."

"Me neither. Do they have any smell left?"

I sniff, and smell only paper. "No, not really."

"Where do you work?" she asks.

"I teach at Merrithew Academy."

From within a slightly less dazzling smile, she lets out a long "Oh." Her eyes looking up at me are wide and I notice, finally, they are brown. "What do you teach?"

"History and Latin."

She's so lovely. Trim and neat in her green coat, the cone of orange roses cradled in one elbow. Chalfont Street slopes more sharply. We cross Chase Street, pass the bakery, the Cafe Suzette, and come to the ivy-covered brick building in the middle of the block.

"This is me," I say.

She looks up at the second story windows. "You live here?"

"Over the candle shop."

"Oh."

"Where do you live?"

"Clementsport. I'm staying with my grandmother."

"I see."

"Well," she says, "Good night."

"Good night. I'll see you tomorrow."

"Tomorrow's Saturday."

"Oh. Right."

"Bon weekend."

"À vous la même."

"Bye." Hoisting her bag higher on her shoulder, she starts off again. I watch the wind pick up the ends of her curls. I stand like a coward and watch her walk away from me, not even knowing her name. Wishing I could explain.

I haven't always been like this, I say to her back. *I was bolder once. Braver. I took chances, I went for it, I wasn't afraid to fail. I didn't fear getting hurt. I had a love I took risks for. My name was hers.*

But you see, she died.

And now I'm afraid of asking for names.

My bones are weary and my throat is full of sadness. I'm turning the key in the lock when I hear someone call, "Hey."

I look. She's at the corner. The light is green but she's

standing still, waving at me from the edge of Baker Street. I look over my shoulder and back. Touch my chest with a fingertip.

Me?

Her head dips back and I can see she's laughing. "I'll see you Monday," she calls.

And I hear my voice answer: "What's your name?"

The air roars in my ears. My heart pounds a fist against the wall of my chest. My toes curl tight in my shoes.

She keeps laughing and yells a name.

I miss it and yell back, "What?"

She jams her roses into an elbow and cups both hands around her mouth. "Jane. What's yours?"

"Tim."

"Good night, Tim."

"Good night, Jane."

Jane.

I roll her name around my mouth like a piece of candy, while in my head, ricocheting off the sides of my skull, is her calling, "Good night, Tim."

Good night, Tim.

Good night, Tim...

SYNCOPE

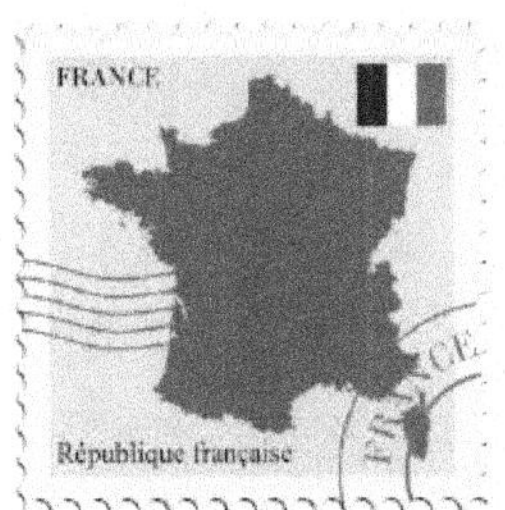

SHE SCREAMED WHEN HE presented her with the two box-seat tickets to the Paris Opera Ballet. Screamed and launched herself at him, arms around his shoulders and legs around his waist. Screamed and kissed every inch of his face as he stumbled backward, narrowly avoiding clonking his head on the sloping eaves. His calf hit the box spring and he fell back onto the mattress with her on his chest. She planted her knees around him, the curtains of her hair closed up his face. With the tickets in one fist and back of his collar in the other, she kissed him hard, gave him her tongue, and growled into his mouth, "You so got yourself a blowjob."

He was all for collecting right then and there, but instead he was promptly abandoned, she was off of him and heading down the little spiral staircase.

"Where you going?" he asked forlornly, following her partway down on the steps. In the small living room she was shrugging into her camel coat and stepping into her boots.

"I have nothing to wear," she said, as if it were the most obvious thing in the world.

"You're gonna leave me hanging?"

She gave him a look as she put on her gloves. "Don't worry, you'll be rewarded. Handsomely."

He tried his best injured expression but she was having none of it.

"Have I ever let you down?" She smiled up at him.

He sighed, capitulated reluctantly. "You are a woman of your word."

"Damn right, sir."

"Fine. Go. Spend a lot of money."

"I will," she said. "Take a nap." With a happy whip of her red cashmere scarf she was heading for the door, off in search of a dress.

"Yes, ma'am," he said, left in the wake of her perfume. He trudged back upstairs and took a moment to admire the view of the 9th arondissement from the picture window before pulling the drapes closed. He lay down on the smooth, cool sheets, reached for a pillow, pounded it into shape. Folding his hands behind his neck he fell asleep, smiling smugly at the slanted ceiling and thinking of all the implications within the word *handsomely*.

Her pleasure that evening was a palpable thing, and it warmed his skin like sunshine. In her new ball gown, with her hair swept back and diamonds winking at her ears, she was so beautiful he found himself quietly choking up. The usher opened the door of their private box with a flourish, bade them enter with a gloved hand. She took two steps in and then stopped dead, open-mouthed. Even he was momentarily stunned at the magnificence. They were top tier, the last box, two birds in a nest. In an awed silence they took in the view of the theatre, the glint and glitter of chandelier light, the velvet seats, the beautiful people below, the orchestra tuning up, and she turned to him with brimming eyes.

"Thank you," she whispered, her hand finding his and squeezing tight. "This is a dream."

She was in her element, sitting up straight and attentive, not wanting to miss a thing. It was a concert-style program this evening, with divertissements from the major classical ballets, interspersed with contemporary works. They opened with two Shakespearian selections: Kenneth MacMillan's iconic balcony scene from *Romeo and Juliet*, followed by John Cranko's comedic pas de deux from *The Taming of the Shrew*. He enjoyed both the performance and her intermittent, whispered commentary. He suspected she was showing off her knowledge a little, touching his wrist and murmuring, "Watch this," a split second before the ballerina made some spectacular leap into her partner's arms. But hell, she did know her art, and she was so happy, he would indulge her anything.

At one beautifully executed passage in *Romeo and Juliet*, she drew in her breath and brought her hands up to enclose her mouth and nose, then folded them into fists beneath her chin and turned her head to smile at him with such bald joy that he was helpless with love for her.

The second act was a contemporary ballet, *Syncope*, which she described as "one of Maurice Béjart's nude mythologies." His interest perked up at that, but within five minutes it deflated like a balloon: the music was dissonant and jarring, the choreography twisted and weird. There was neither myth nor any discernible storyline, and frankly the nudity was nothing to scream at.

Confused, he sat back, put an ankle on the other knee, crossed his arms over his chest and looked over at her questioningly. She sat back as well, returned the expression and rolled her eyes.

He smiled, suffused with forgiving affection, and he put his palm on her face, running his thumb along her cheekbone, curling his fingertips under her jaw. She turned her mouth into his palm, then her eyes turned wicked and she closed her lips around his thumb.

At the touch of her tongue he felt a stirring below the belt and raised his eyebrows at her. She flicked her gaze to the closed box door, back to him, and in a rustle of silk and tulle she slid off her seat and was on her knees beside his chair.

"Stop," he said, with *stop* being the furthest thing from his mind.

"Shh."

"You're insane," he whispered slowly, keeping his arms crossed but taking his ankle off its perch and letting her move in closer.

"I believe I owe you for the tickets." Her fingers were at his belt buckle, undoing him. He swallowed and ran a hand down the curve of her neck, out over her bare shoulders. Surreptitiously he turned his head this way and that. Nobody sat above them, and the high partitions blocked the next box from view. Only the people on the other side of the ring might have a clue what was going on, but they seemed transfixed by the performance. Nobody was looking.

"Is there a lock on that door?" he asked with the last vestiges of rational thought he could drum up.

"Doubt it," she whispered, unzipping him, reaching into his pants. And then she had him in her hands, he was fully hard and completely turned on and...

Fuck it.

He exhaled softly, closed his eyes and let his head tilt back—*fuck everything*—and she was down on him in the dark of the Paris Opera during a performance and his life *(yes)* was complete.

The music became tolerable. He opened his eyes and stared at the complex, weaving patterns of bodies onstage, and it all made sense. It was all just *great.*

Her mouth was all over him, drawing him down into that warm, wet softness beyond her tongue and teeth, pulling and releasing, again and again. If they were in bed she would be holding him down, working him with both hands and mouth in that way she had with him. If they were alone he would be groaning his head off, telling her anything and everything. But here and now he could only sit still and project normalcy and not give away what was going on beyond the balcony wall. And it was going to send him right over the edge. Fast.

Slowly he ran his hand over her, wherever he could reach. Her skin so soft, her mouth was so good. She had him. Damn this woman and her ways, she always had him, she knew just how to make him crazy.

She wasn't letting up. The music swelled into crescendo, the dancers grew more frenzied. As did her head in his lap. Was she actually choreographing this? He wouldn't put it past her. God, her mouth, her tongue, her hands, her skin. With a dissonant blast from the brass section, it was on him then and he closed his eyes and held his face still as the wave crashed over him. His heart pounding hard in his ears, toes curling in his dress shoes, hand curling hard into her shoulder. The roll of her collarbone between his thumb and fingers as he flooded her mouth and she took it, took all he had to give, she was good, she was so damn good...

Interminable minutes slipped by. Their breathing stilled in unison. She was still kneeling between his feet, now with her cheek resting on his leg and her eyes closed, one of her hands curled in one of his. He held it tight and with his other he tucked a loose strand of hair behind her ear. Tenderly traced her jaw, her diamonds, the slope of her neck and shoulder, the line of her rising and falling breasts. Quietly she put him back together, zipped and buckled him, and slipped demurely back into her seat just as the music faded out and the lights onstage went dim.

The theatre filled with applause. They clapped along enthusiastically, and when the stage lights came up they looked just once at each other and dissolved into hushed, complicit laughter.

He leaned in close to her ear. "Have I mentioned how intensely in love with you I am?"

"Mm-hm," she murmured, eyes fixed on the stage again, face twitching from the attempt to look composed and the color rising up in her neck.

Throughout the rest of his life, if ever he found himself in a conversation about dance, he took great pleasure in opining that his favorite ballet was *Syncope*, which he'd had the privilege of seeing at the Paris Opera. One of Béjart's nude mythologies. Really intense but not overly-sexualized. Incredible, really. He didn't have the words to do it justice. You had to see it live. It would just *blow* your mind.

And if she happened to be standing by him, she blushed every time.

SHORT FOR?

A Train between Buffalo and New York City

An unexpected turn of events landed Sam Ponzinaro in Upstate New York for Thanksgiving. The reunion of his college housemates was supposed to be in Vermont, but at the last minute, Dashiel Slay had a setback. He was too weak to travel, would it be all right if everyone came to him instead? His parents' house in Dunkirk had more than enough room and he'd be so grateful.

He was irresistible, even more so with his failing health and his newfound means of expression. The four other friends, who never could deny Dash anything, scrambled and rearranged their travel plans, re-orienting toward the shores of Lake Erie.

They had enough snow to be festive, not enough to be a hassle. Dash ran a lowgrade fever on Thanksgiving morning, so the gang built snowmen outside the living room window, where Dash could watch from his bundled-up recline on the couch. They fell easily into their old touchy-feely ways, draping and cuddling and snuggling like a pack of puppies.

"I'm so glad you came," Dash said, over and over.

After days of feasting and sloth, everyone piled in the car to take Sam to the Exchange Street station on Saturday morning. They kissed and hugged him, ruffled his hair, slapped his ass. Sam lugged his duffel up the slushy steps and turned to wave one last time at his friends. They stood in tableaux, huddled together in the gently-falling snow, tousled and yawning.

Dash stood in his rightful, alpha place at the center of the pack. His leather jacket was unzipped to show a fire-engine red T-shirt. He'd pulled his shoulder-length blond hair into a tail, revealing the blue streaks beneath. Against the industrial gray Buffalo morning, he was a rare, tropical bird. Through the forest of waving hands and blown kisses, he solemnly gave Sam the finger.

"Bite me," Sam mouthed through the snowflakes. And then aloud, "Zip your jacket, you moron."

His throat was tight around the words. Moving into the car, he pretended he wasn't so bittersweet and confused on this dank November morning. Pretended it was no big deal Dash had come into his bed last night.

He took the first vacant seat he saw, but after five minutes, he realized he'd situated himself in front two whining children and across the aisle from their exhausted parents. He couldn't stand it. He needed peace. He put his jacket back on, took down his bag and moved. He had to shlep through three cars before finding a center section with two seats facing two seats.

Paused a few feet away, Sam smiled. Sometimes you found yourself in situations, and you didn't know how, you didn't know why. You just accepted it and said thank you.

Three of the seats were empty. A guy slept in the fourth.

And he was hot.

"Thank you," Sam whispered. He hauled his bag up to the overhead rack and carefully stepped over the stranger's outstretched legs to get to the window seat. He unzipped his jacket and blew on his chilled hands, assessing his new travel companion with quiet relish.

What have we here?

His facial features were youthful, but his brown hair was lightly threaded with gray at his temples. Combed back from a high forehead, a brow crisply bisected by dark eyebrows and sloping to meet a strong, straight nose. Bits of silver in the five o'clock shadow creeping across his chin and jaw. Olive skin. Cheekbones you could sharpen a knife on. Full mouth a little slack with sleep.

The train jolted and the man's body shifted, his head now tilting to the shoulder. From out of the collar of his maroon-and-green sweater tumbled a gold chain with a cross. His arms were wrapped around his torso, ankles crossed. He wore scuffed, muddy work boots. Sam wanted to look at his hands, but they were hidden somewhere in his armpits.

Eyes stuffed full, Sam poked around in his backpack and took out his new magic markers and coloring book. Both were a gag gift from Dashiel that Sam opened with delight and took quite seriously. He did so much work on the computer these days. It was years since he'd colored by hand. Years since he'd had a brand-new set of medium-tipped felt pens in 48 brilliant colors.

Sam ran a palm over the book's glossy cover: *The Marvel Superheroes Coloring Book*. He and Dash were comic book junkies. It was what drew them together in college. Art and graphic novels first. Followed by other things.

Last night, Dash brought the markers into Sam's bed. He wore two pairs of socks and fingerless gloves. He wrapped a string of Christmas lights around his head like an electric crown of thorns. Then went to work penning giants on Sam's shoulder blades. Elves climbing up his spine. Pegasi wrapping mighty wings around his ribcage. Axe-wielding warriors on his chest. A wizard on his stomach. And then...

"Dude, no," Sam said, laughing as Dash pulled his sweats down. "Stop."

"Let me," Dash said, pushing strands of blue and gold behind his ears. In the garland lights, the color was up high along his cheekbones. Always his creativity shone on his face, blooming like a fever when he was in the flow.

"Dude, that *tickles*," Sam said, writhing.

"Hold still."

"You're drawing on my *dick*. This is beyond weird. Even for us."

"But you're letting me," Dash said around the cap

held in his teeth. "Because you love me. Shh, stop squirming. Focus on your breathing and it won't tickle as much."

Sam lay still, toes clenched and breathing deeply. Feeling the color build up in his own face when he started to get hard.

"Huh," Dash said. "This was going to be a dagger. Now it has to be a broadsword."

"Quiet, you," Sam said softly. He reached to run his hand along Dash's jaw. Dash turned his face into the touch, nudging like a cat. The light pooled in the hollow beneath his cheekbones. He was so thin now. Half the man he used to be. Eyes perpetually shadowed. The once sculpted body frail and failing.

"Thanks for coming," he said. "I loved having everyone, but I really wanted you."

They held eyes a long time, Sam lightly stroking his friend's face. "I want you to be all right."

"I'll be mostly right." As he shifted from one elbow to the other, a flicker of discomfort passed through his gaunt face.

"How bad is the pain?" Sam asked.

"It's manageable."

"Don't be brave for me."

Dash made a dismissive grunt as he switched markers. "I'm just tired all the time. The kind of tired that makes you stupid." As he looked down at the mural on Sam's body, his crown of lights slid sideways. "And I don't have much of a sex drive anymore. I mean, in case you..."

"Don't," Sam said softly, the room swimming warm and wet.

"I don't have any condoms anyway." Dash raised an eyebrow. "Me. No condoms. They also reported snow in hell this morning."

"I didn't come here to sleep with you," Sam said.

Brows pulled down tight, Dash drew back a little. "*What?*"

Sam reached and knocked the lights away, then the markers. "Get over here, asshole."

Dash came army-crawling up the mattress. He snuggled up tight and Sam tucked the covers around their bodies.

"No," he said softly when Dash's hand closed around his penis and gave a knowledgeable stroke and an expert squeeze.

"I don't mind." His laugh blew warm on the side of Sam's neck. "I mean, my cock doesn't work so well these days but I still know what to do with one. Particularly yours."

Sam reached beneath the blankets and twined their fingers. "I just want to hold onto you right now."

"You dating someone?"

"I wouldn't be in bed with you if I was."

"You should be."

"In bed with you?"

"No. Dating someone. *With* someone. I hate seeing all your Sam-ness go to waste."

Sam ran the heel of his hand roughly over each eye.

"I think I liked you better when you were a heartless prick."

"I really was a prick to you."

Sam shrugged the shoulder Dash was using as a pillow. "Doesn't matter anymore."

"It does." Dash's arm across Sam's chest pulled tighter. "And I'm sorry."

"Quiet, you."

Little humming sighs as Sam ran fingers through Dash's hair. Stroked the little soft hollow behind his ear. Scratched along the unreachable edges of his shoulder blades. All the secret sweet spots Sam knew, having collected them during their one romantic year together.

"Feels good to hold you," Dash said.

Sam kissed his head. "Go to sleep."

They held each other all night. In the morning, the ink on Sam's skin had rubbed off like bruises onto Dash's skin and smeared rainbows on the sheets.

"I like you messing them up this way," Dash said, grinning.

"Quiet, you..."

The train rocked Sam to and fro within the memories. Coloring superheroes, he was alone in his head with Dash on his skin. So engrossed in activity and lost in memory, he didn't know how much time had gone by when the sleeping prince in the opposite seat finally woke up.

He did it with a sudden intake of breath. His eyes stayed shut as he stretched, grandly, digging the heels of his hands by his ears and pushing his elbows toward the dome of the car. Then he yawned, rubbing his chest through his sweater.

He looked like a puppy. No, a bear. A young, sturdy, well-fed bear awaking from a nap. He opened his eyes, saw Sam looking and smiled shyly, ducking behind his lids.

"Welcome back," Sam said.

The bear smiled again, proudly now, eyes shut and giving another uncontrollable, high-elbowed stretch. "Good to be here."

His voice was soft, a little husky in the back of his throat, as if he had a cold. He shook his head, cracked his knuckles and drew the hair back from his forehead with the palms of his tan hands. "Wow," he said. "I feel like eighteen bucks and change."

"How'd you feel when you fell asleep?"

"Like a student loan."

"That's some improvement."

"Wait until I get a shower." He tilted his head from side to side, working the kinks out of his neck.

Feeling the first stirrings of immediate and undeniable physical attraction, Sam pictured him in the shower, the warm water and soapsuds running in white rivulets across his skin and chest hair and hard compact muscles. He instantly liked this guy's body and the way he occupied space so cozily. Sitting with his arms crossed again, one ankle now hitched over the other knee, he seemed solid and immutable in a way that was sensuous.

He stared at nothing, long lashes blinking over his eyes, and Sam sensed this was someone who, like him, could be perfectly happy being left alone with his thoughts.

He also sensed, on a more inherent level, this was someone who was probably nothing less than a sensational lover.

And probably someone who was straight.

Oh well, can't have everything.

The bear gave a start and leaned across the empty seat beside him to look out the window. "Oh man," he muttered, and glanced at Sam. "Where are we?"

"Just outside Rochester. Did you miss your stop?"

His eyebrows wrinkled. "What time is it?"

Sam informed him it was a quarter of three, but he still looked troubled.

"What day is it?"

"Saturday."

He gave his shy smile again. "Thanks."

Sam wondered how long he had been traveling that he'd lost track of the days, but said nothing. He lowered his head back to his coloring and willed himself not to look across. He also told the interest sensor on his gaydar to knock it off.

"I'm gonna get some coffee," the guy said. "You want some?"

"I don't drink coffee," Sam said.

The gentle beast's gaze narrowed for an instant, then softened. "Tea? Water?"

Sam's gaydar crossed its arms and raised a smug

eyebrow.

"Tea's good." Sam leaned back to dig for his wallet, though he had the confidant and victorious feeling that he was being treated.

"No, no, I got it," the guy said, and headed down the aisle, holding onto the backs of seats for balance. Once he was gone, Sam imagined Dash popping over the back of the seat to give an exuberant high five. *It's on, baby.*

Sam smiled through the air at his friend's invisible, tangible presence. A multi-layered emotion pressed him on all sides.

I wish you were here.

Well, no, I don't. Not here right now with your big mouth and irresistible charm that doesn't give anyone else a chance.

But I want you to be in the world.

I don't want you to die...

"Here you go." The bear had returned and was handing Sam a hot paper cup. "I got it with milk, hope that's all right."

"That's fine." Sam peered in the paper bag now being held out to him. It was resourcefully stuffed full of Domino packets. "But I think we'll need more sugar."

"I know, I overdid it. As usual." Perched on his seat, he removed the lid of his coffee, added sugar, stirred and sipped. "By the way, I'm Ned."

"Short for?"

"Edward." He added another sugar to his coffee.

"I'm Sam."

"Short for?"

"Nothing. Just Sam." He had to move his work aside before he could remove, add, stir, and sip. Ned leaned across the space between their seats to see what Sam had been up to.

"Wow," he said. "Great markers."

"They were an early Christmas present."

Ned's fingertips ran across the spectrum of colors. "Makes me think of grade school. Beginning of the year when you had a brand new pack. All the colors, no caps missing."

"It's got such potential."

"This is cool, too." Ned fanned the pages of the coloring book, keeping his coffee at a cautious distance.

"Also a present." Sam crossed his ankles on the empty seat across. "You going to New York?"

"No. Well, I'll have to change trains in New York, but I'm going to Philadelphia."

"Ah."

The conversation halted. Ned didn't ask where Sam was going, and Sam, all at once, didn't feel like *working* this encounter. He was tired.

The kind of tired that makes you stupid.

Ned stared out the window, swirling the coffee around in the cup before sipping. Sam watched his Adam's apple bob a few times, then turned to the window himself, uninterested in coloring any more.

The train passed clusters of houses. Many of them had every window lit up and four cars in the driveway.

Others were dark, abandoned for the holiday. Loneliness sat in Sam's lap. He'd been first to leave the party. He imagined the gang sitting cozily around the fire, munching two-day old turkey sandwiches. Sara would be at the piano, picking out a Chopin nocturne. Marie would be reading. Carston and Zack playing Scrabble. Dashiel would be drawing, the color up high in his face. Or he'd be sleeping on the coach, his blue-and-blond hair caught in the light from the hearth, skin like burnished gold.

Sam's chilly fingers unconsciously rubbed together as he imagined plunging his hand into the thick hair covering the nape of Dash's neck. It was the warmest place he knew. On how many winter nights had he thrust his cold hands into that mane of hair to thaw them? When had cupping the back of Dash's head ceased to be a means of warming his fingers, and started becoming something more? When had Dash stopped being merely amused by the gesture, and started nudging his head more insistently against Sam's touch?

Sam ran his fingertips across the magic markers, lined up in variegated order. Blush-rose to ruby, lemon to ochroid, lime to olive. He heard words, but it was a moment before he realized Ned had said something.

Sam blinked. "Sorry?"

"Are you going to New York?" Ned's right eyelid was a hair lower than his left, making his gaze the tiniest bit lopsided.

"Yeah."

"Live there?"

Sam nodded. "I was having Thanksgiving with friends in Buffalo."

"Oh."

"Where did you get on?"

"Toronto."

"Long ride. No wonder you didn't know what day it was."

"I was suppose to fly. My flight got cancelled."

"Bummer."

"Eh?" Ned shrugged. "It's not the end of the world." His coffee finished, he was slouched way down, feet crossed next to Sam's seat. "What do you do?"

"I'm a graphic designer."

"Comic strips?"

Sam laughed. "No. Commercial design, mostly. How about you?"

"Getting my master's in biochemistry. I'm doing a research internship at the Lankenau Institute."

"Sounds exciting."

Ned's smile was sheepish. "On paper. In reality I'm a glorified grunt and it's a lot of data entry."

"Are you working on a specific study?"

"Right now I'm analyzing data on people with HIV-related neuromuscular complications."

Sam went cold all over. The shock must've shown in his face because Ned tilted his chin and his lopsided gaze settled deeper in Sam's. The moment swelled between them like a gamble.

Sam licked his lips. "Friend of mine is going through that," he said.

"Yeah?"

"The guy whose place I was at for Thanksgiving, actually. He was my housemate in college."

"I see," Ned said, playing with the cross on his gold chain. "When was he diagnosed?"

"With HIV? He was two years out of college. Closer to three. His boyfriend fucked around on him. They both ended up positive."

"Jesus," Ned said, wincing.

"It was under control for a long while. He was on this drug called Hart and... What?"

Ned's pinched face had smoothed out and was now broad with a gentle smile and something that looked like affection. "HAART," he said, spelling out the letters. "Highly active antiretroviral therapy. It's not one drug, it's a regimen. But that's not the point. Sorry. I interrupted. It was being managed and then?"

It took Sam a beat to disengage from Ned's smile and find where he left off. "He got sick over the summer. Something with a really long complex name I can't pronounce. It goes by something shorter that sounds French but I forget what it is."

"Guillan-Barré?"

The evil name was elegant in Ned's mouth. Sam stared, then looked away, shaking his head. "Yeah."

"I trip over the technical name, too. Demyelinating polyrad...polyridiculous something or other. Don't tell my boss."

Sam pinched thumb and forefinger and drew them across his lips.

Ned tugged at an earlobe. "Anyway, I'm sorry, man."

"I don't suppose you have any miraculous, groundbreaking news to share from the study?"

"I could tell you, but then I'd have to kill you."

"Naturally."

Ned smiled. He had the nicest face. He was a campfire of steady assurance, making you want to roll up a log and sit by him. Let him crackle and pop in your ears and warm you.

"I couldn't draw any conclusions for you at this point anyway," he was saying. "But if it makes you feel better, the focus of HIV studies is shifting because the disease has gone from a death sentence to a chronic condition. AIDS patients are living longer lives than ever. We're analyzing data from people in their forties and fifties. We couldn't do that before. Get what I'm saying?"

Sam nodded. His hands itched to reach toward the flames.

"Your friend will have to manage this all his life. He'll be susceptible to all kinds of secondary complications. But we know what those are. And we have the data from people who are living with them. Living into their fifties, even sixties. I don't know if that helps ease your mind any, but..."

"It does."

"How was your friend when you saw him?"

"Tired. Tired and weak. But we were all there. The five of us who used to live together, I mean. It was good. He loved it." Sam's voice gummed up at the back of his tongue. He cleared his throat roughly and looked out the window.

"Connection is key, man," Ned said. "No drug can replace that. Still, it's hard watching someone you love suffer. And struggle. You got my heart on that one."

"Sometimes the struggle is harder to watch than the suffering," Sam heard himself say above the thud of his heart. "He was one of those guys that..."

"That what?"

Sam looked at him. He pulled at the connection between them and found it taut. He pushed at this serendipitous meeting and found it tough. He leaned on the moment a little. Then a little more. And found he trusted it.

"Dash was one of those buddies you meet and it's like, *Where the fuck you been all my life? Been looking for you everywhere.* He had his own force of gravity. Wherever he was, that's where people wanted to be. We were like best friends in five minutes." Sam drew in a breath, distilled the courage within it and went on. "And then shit happened and we ended up together a little while."

"Where was this?"

"Rhode Island School of Design."

"Was it easy to be out there?"

A beat while Sam chewed on the question. "It was

easy if you had a tribe. Or easier. Relatively speaking."

"I did two years of undergrad at Catholic University in DC," Ned said. "It wasn't easy, needless to say. Tribe or no tribe."

Their eyes held through a vulnerable, blinking moment. Sam nodded. Slowly Ned's head mirrored. Understanding flowed across the space between them.

Where you been? Sam thought.

"So you were together a little while?" Ned said, prompting.

"Junior year. But he caused me more grief as a lover than I could handle. He had a golden heart but when it came to love he was ham-fisted. We were better as friends. Or at least, I was better off being just friends. But anyway. He was always so invincible. He had this energy. His name totally suited him. Dash."

"Short for?"

"Dashiel. He was just...*dashing*, you know?"

Ned's chin lifted once then lowered.

Sam gave a dismissive shrug. "But enough about me."

The gentle smile was back on Ned's face. "We weren't talking about you."

Sam drank his tea. It was lukewarm and too sweet. "It's just really strange meeting you. Today of all days. Strange and random."

"They say things happen for a reason."

"I've heard that."

"Are you hungry?" Ned said.

"Me? I don't know. Maybe a little."

"There's a great place a few cars up. Loads of ambience."

* * * * *

THEIR FIRST MEAL TOGETHER consisted of microwaved cheeseburgers, soggy fries and three beers apiece. They loitered quite a while in the smoky club car, and when they returned to their seats, the train was winding its way in and out of Syracuse. They sat down in their original seats, opposite one another.

Later, looking back, Sam couldn't remember all the words. There were too many. He and Ned talked and talked. Snark, innuendo and jokes bantered between them, enough to feel flirtatious. But no obvious come-ons or physical overtures. Sam's gaydar gave up trying to figure out what the hell was going on. He was beyond looking to score by now. He was enjoying the ride and the company at face value. He and Ned had read a ton of the same books. The concert resumes aligned and they could quote the same movies. Ned was better traveled. He told some tales about his youth hostel circuit in Europe. And a horrific excursion to Japan where absolutely everything that could go wrong did.

Sam listened and laughed, liking the way Ned told stories, describing people and rehashing dialogue. He was bright, and had a glib, sarcastic edge to his humor that would've been somewhat obnoxious if he hadn't included himself in the barbs.

Where you been all my life? Sam thought in the comfortable silences.

It was around the time the train reached Albany when Ned got up to use the bathroom, and when he came back, he sat down in the seat beside Sam.

"Can I?" he asked.

Sam thought he meant taking the seat. Then he saw Ned pointing to the coloring book and markers.

"Help yourself," Sam said, passing them over.

Watching Ned color in the Hulk, with the rumble of the tracks beneath them, Sam grew sleepy. Finally he dozed off in the car's rocking embrace, his head against the window. The edges of his mind unraveled, his chest open and his stomach calm. Then the train gave a hard lurch and he woke with a surprised grunt. Ned reached, caught Sam's cheek gently in the palm of his hand, and drew Sam's head down to his shoulder.

"Come here," he said softly.

Sam went limp and allowed his body to lean against Ned. Eyes closed, he sensed Ned capping markers, closing the metal box and placing it and the book on the opposite seat. Then Sam's hand was suddenly enveloped in warmth, pressed between both of Ned's.

"I'm sorry about your friend," Ned said.

"Thanks," Sam whispered, eyes still closed. Ned was rubbing the ragged edges of Sam's fingernails. His mouth brushed Sam's fingers and his exhaled breath was a warm sigh on Sam's knuckles.

They held hands all the way to Penn Station.

The rest happened with wonderful spontaneity and an astonishing mutual clarity of what they wanted. It was 10:00 and Sam's train to Philadelphia did not leave until 11:30.

"Want to go for a drink?" Sam asked.

"Sure."

They found a T.G.I. Friday's and shared some potato skins. Back at Penn Station, they exchanged business cards.

"This was good," Sam said. "If I'd stayed the extra day, I never would've met you."

Ned's teeth caught his bottom lip, then let go. "I like this story."

Sam slapped Ned's upper arm lightly. Slid his hand to Ned's shoulder and squeezed. Then moved further against his bristly cheek. Ned turned his mouth into Sam's palm and exhaled.

"This goodbye got hard all of a sudden," he murmured.

"I know."

Ned let his duffel bag slide off his shoulder to the floor. He took Sam's face in both his hands and kissed him.

"You're not making this easier," Sam whispered.

"Story of my life."

They lingered, kissing, until the second call squawked from the PA.

"Boooo-aard!" echoed the conductor. "Seven minutes to board!"

"I don't want to get on the train," Ned said as they hugged. Each one's fists pressed against the other's shoulder blades. "Shit."

Sam gathered his courage. "What if I got on it with you?"

Ned leaned back. "What?"

Sam shrugged. "It's only Saturday. I'm enjoying you. Let's keep going."

Ned stared, half a smile on his surprised lips. "This is crazy," he finally said.

"Does that mean yes? Hurry up if I'm going to make it to the ticket window and back."

"I'll buy your ticket."

"No, I will," Sam said. "My treat."

KAIKOURA

Tipene te Kanae spoke English perfectly well. He spoke many languages well. His father had sent him to an immersion school where only te reo Maori was spoken, thus he was fluent in an ancient tongue which had been discouraged after World War II, revitalized and declared one of New Zealand's official languages in 1987. And yet, despite the resurgence of immersion education from the Kohanga Reo movement, it was spoken by less than five percent of the population.

His mother spoke Vietnamese, of course. She was one of the 412 original boat people admitted to New Zealand in 1977. She was well-educated with a passion for languages and a good ear. On any given day she would lapse into English or French or Chinese, and was currently trying to master Russian.

All this gave Tip a huge advantage in his business of running boat tours off the Kaikoura Peninsula. Or rather, it would have, had he been socially inclined toward tourists. He cared little for advantage, and cared less for social niceties. Fluent in multiple languages, he preferred not to speak at all, although the truth was as a writer, people interested him. He collected characters.

Only appearing aloof and reserved, he possessed near total recall, was keenly observant at best and a pathological snoop at worst. Pretending not to understand his customers allowed him to openly eavesdrop on their conversations, and at the end of the workday he either took his findings home and carefully transcribed them into a journal, or he took them to the local bar where his reputation as a storyteller preceded him.

The bookings were handled by his assistant Hannah. (Her name was Airini but she Westernized it during the summer, encouraging him to do the same and change Tipene to Steven. Needless to say the advice went unheeded.) Tip never knew who he was taking or where to until Hannah put the itinerary into his hands. So it neither surprised nor concerned him today's last run would carry only a single couple, and when he saw them waiting on the dock, it was no surprise it was the Americans.

They had come with him before: two days ago to see the fur seals, and just yesterday to whale watch. They had captured Tip's interest right away, for not only was their attraction to each other a fascinating and intensely palpable thing, but as a couple they seemed to attract the rest of the passengers. On both cruises it had happened: wherever they went on the boat, others longed to follow.

Whatever place they settled was the place to be.

Ironic, Tip thought, for clearly the one thing these two loved best was to be solely with each other. The man, especially, revolved around his lover like a satellite, leading Tip to privately refer to him as Marama, which meant "moon." He often made up names for his passengers this way, but not always in flattery. It seemed he, too, had fallen under the spell of this couple, who, when they locked gazes, made the sun surge brighter overhead.

Tip drew on his sunglasses as he walked down the dock, nodding curtly to them.

"Tipene," the woman said as he passed, which made his step falter. Rarely did he hand out his name to his customers and he didn't recall doing so with her. But she knew his. How? Had she overheard it? Eavesdropped? He looked back and smiled, something he did even more rarely on the job, and with a small gesture indicated they were welcome to board.

His gaze followed the woman, whom he had not yet named. If the man was Marama, the moon, then she should be Whenua, which meant "earth." Her eyes were an intense blue-green, like a jeweled planet, but Tip didn't think Whenua suited her. It was a fat woman's name. This woman was thin, even skinny, but no such term existed in Maori and he hated it in English. Skinny was a mean word.

He regarded his female passenger, finding no meanness. She was slender, not skinny. Slender was a good word in English. Sexy, even. It conjured up an instant sensation of small but lush, solid weight in your arms. It slid around your mouth like a piece of hard candy. Slender.

Slender as a blade.

The simile pleasant and sweet on his tongue, Tip opened throttle and headed out to sea, the peninsula unfolding in all its breathtaking beauty as they left the dock. The day had been fine and clear, the peaks of the Southern Alps visible in spectacular detail, looming in violet and white majesty over the bay. Now clouds began to gather at the peaks, turning faintly orange and pink as the sun changed angles in the sky.

Tip was pleased: he knew the dolphin pods well and sunset was a good time to swim. Cold, but that was what the wetsuits were for. He didn't say a word to the Americans, who seemed equally content not to engage with him. It was not unkindness, just a simple realization the people here had their preferences. Tip wanted his time to observe. They only wanted each other.

From behind tinted lenses and an unreadable face, Tip watched the lovers. She, still nameless, sat on one of the bulkheads and Marama sat on the deck between her feet, his elbows draped over her knees. Tip lowered his sunglasses a little, squinting at the woman's leg, suntanned the creamy brown of an egg. A long scar ran from the bump of her knee joint nearly to her ankle. A startling vein of pink quartz in the smooth skin. Marama's fingers caressed it as his chin lolled on his chest. The woman had her hands on his shoulders and was pressing her thumbs along his spine. Skillfully she took his head in one hand, moving it here, turning it there, her other hand pressing, kneading up the back of his neck and then down between his shoulder blades again.

Tip rolled his own head around in empathy, divining her touch. She had good hands. She was strong. Strong, slender and scarred.

Strong heart, Tip mused, trying out and rejecting various nouns and adjectives. *Strong hands.*

Kaha meant strength but it was too clumsy for a name. He kept coming back to slender as a blade. He liked it. The curve of her calf was like a Samurai sword. The long scar could easily be a battle wound. And in bed she could probably get both legs around your back and...

He smiled. Yes. He would call her Haori, which meant "sword."

Forty-five minutes offshore, above the underwater canyon that stretched down over sixteen hundred metres, Tip maneuvered the boat to the approximate place he knew from both experience and instinct where the dusky dolphins would come at sunset. From his captain's chair he brought up his binoculars and scanned the horizon patiently. No sign of a pod.

He looked back to the stern: Marama and Haori were changing, donning their thick wetsuits, masks and snorkels. They seemed to know what they were doing. No doubt Hannah had drilled them well.

Tip raised his binoculars once more. There. Moving

south. A pod, close to two hundred by his guess.

"Papahu!" he called out, not taking his eyes from the creatures who were beginning their antics. Of all the dolphin species, duskies were the most acrobatic and social. Blatant show-offs.

Tip turned in his chair. Marama was watching the dolphins, open-mouthed, both hands pressed to his head. Haori was looking back at Tip, her turquoise eyes huge, the whole of her body tense with anticipation. Again, Tip was moved to smile at her, then he flicked the back of his hand at both of them, indicating "Go!"

They moved as one, pulling their masks down, snatching hands and leaping into the cold blue of the open sea. The combined splash of their bodies set off a chain reaction. The water around the boat was filled with dolphins, fins breaking the surface, shiny grey bodies launching. It seemed even they could not resist the gravitational pull of this man and woman. Tip left his seat and lounged against the starboard side, watching intently.

Swimming with dolphins was always a profound experience, and over the years he had seen every kind of reaction from hysterical weeping to uncontrollable laughter. He had seen elderly women scream without a shred of inhibition as dolphins arced over their heads. He had seen the most hard-hearted man's man reduced to a humbled, tearful wreck after coming face to face with a dusky. Young and old, they all left Tip's boat altered by the encounter. "Amazing" was a word thrown around a lot as they stumbled ashore.

Amazing. Dude, that was amazing. That was the most amazing thing that ever happened to me. Ever. Dude. Amazing.

Hannah would lecture customers to remember the dolphins were wild creatures. This wasn't Sea World where they were trained to be on-demand entertainers. In their own habitat, they were the ones making the demands, like entitled teenagers, and if you bored them, they would move on. You had to keep them amused and Marama was proving to be a pro at it: splashing around, diving often, talking and singing out loud, blowing streamers of water out the end of his snorkel. Haori was attempting to do the same, but she was laughing too hard. She spit out her own snorkel, pulled up her mask and treaded water, laughing helplessly, the sound echoing back to Tip's ears. Duskies sliced through the water all around her, clicking and huffing, wanting her to play.

Marama surfaced and pulled up his own mask, honing in on his lover. Tip squinted and raised the binoculars. Two circular fields of vision merged into one. Marama had Haori's face in his hands and he was kissing her. They were both breathing hard from the effort to keep treading. Tip imagined the heat of her mouth, salty with icy ocean water, the juxtaposition of heat and cold against his mouth. He felt the heave of her lungs for air, for more of his air, and how her jaw and cheekbones would roll against his palms. He wanted to trap their passion like pinning a butterfly specimen to velvet. They would leave forever after this trip, but he could keep this moment.

Still kissing, the couple sank beneath the surface, sending up a soufflé of bubbles. All around where they had just been, the sleek, domed heads of duskies popped up. The humans resurfaced, laughing again, and in a cacophony of squeaks, chatters and clicks, the dolphins scattered.

The pod moved on. Marama and Haori climbed aboard the boat and Tip set out to follow. They got in four good swims before Tip judged both the angle of the setting sun and the chatter of Haori's teeth, and deemed it time to go. Once his charges were safely aboard, he pulled the makeshift curtain, giving them privacy to use the hot water hose and change into dry clothes.

Accompanied by a cloud of cape petrels and another pod of duskies, Tip took his boat in. Marama stood in the stern, strong and windblown in sunglasses, Haori held tight in his arms. He moved his chin, then his mouth over top of her head. She was soft and small in her shorts and sweater. Her hair, Tip noticed, had been sleek and straight at the start of the trip but was now drying into rippled waves. Her hand moved up and down Marama's back. She tilted up her chin to look at him. He turned his head to look down at her. The sun surged in the rosy sky. Tip lowered his sunglasses and watched them kiss.

Once docked, they thanked him profusely. Then Marama went to square things with Hannah, leaving

Haori on the dock, leaning her foot and forearms on the rail and looking back out to sea. Tip's eyebrows lowered in consternation as he noticed a second long scar running down the inside of her calf. And further up, above her knee, a cruel-looking starburst of puckered flesh on her inner thigh.

Three wounds to the leg.

Tipene te Kanae, who had no care for social niceties, approached this female warrior on reverent feet. As he set his own elbows on the rail, he felt as audacious and reckless as if he were slipping into bed beside her.

Haori didn't move a muscle or turn a hair in his direction. "That was amazing," she said.

He nodded, wanting to ask her name but overcome with shyness.

"We didn't talk to you much," she said. "I hope we weren't rude." Her hand came up to toy with her necklace, a thin chain off which hung a small pearl and a tiny gold fish.

Tip swallowed. "What are you called?"

"Daisy," she said.

He looked at her. "Daisy? The flower?"

She nodded, pulling her hair back from her face. "Do you have them in New Zealand?"

"Of course. Tikumu," he said. "Mountain daisy. What happened to your leg?"

Then she turned her head. Looked at him with those blue-green eyes. A flush of sunburn on her cheekbones. A smattering of freckles across the bridge of her nose.

She was proud, brave and lovely.

"Long story," she said, smiling. "And long ago."

"Happy ending?" he asked. Her smile widened, and her elbow bumped his as if they had passed a private joke.

"Happy beginning."

Tip thought up and rejected a half-dozen responses. He hardly knew what he wanted to say. She had touched him. Her eyes and her scars and her untold story moved him. She was a dolphin arcing over his head, leaving him humbled to speech instead of silence.

"I'm glad you could come again today," he said, his voice caught up and gruff in his throat.

"I loved it." She pushed off the railing with an easy, unconscious grace. "Thank you."

"Kia kaha," he said softly. She wrinkled her eyebrows and, in one of the few times in his life, he explained himself. "It means stay strong."

"Kia kaha," she repeated. Perfectly. Like his mother, she had a good ear. She smiled at him, raised her hand briefly in farewell, and then walked away to where Marama was waiting for her. She dug him in the side playfully, he dodged, then wound his arm around her, pulling her in tight, his hand disappearing in her wind-tangled hair.

As the Moon and the Sword left the dock, Tipene te Kanae lifted his sunglasses from his eyes and longed to follow.

Naked as Birth

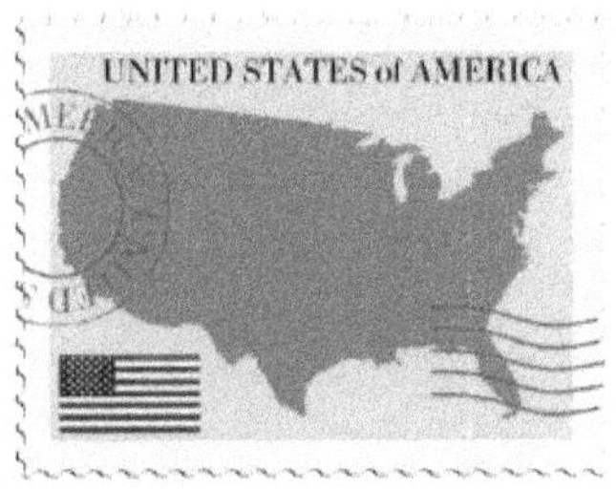

"Are you ready?" Chen asks.

"Yeah." My throat's so dry, the word gets stuck and I just nod the rest.

He kisses me. "Don't be afraid."

I'm shaking crazy nervous, every hair on my body screaming *Holy shit, I'm really doing this.* But I'm not *afraid.* I'm ready to not like it. I'm prepared to change my mind. It could be great, or it could be nothing more than weird. But it's nothing to be afraid of. I know that much.

Chen finishes rolling the condom down and moves on his knees between my legs. I can feel the heat coming off him. It presses on me, dry and hollow like a sauna. Crackling and woodsy in my nose and throat.

His hands skim lightly over my stomach. "Can't fucking believe this," he says, softer than air. His face is magic. Like he's watching the birth of a sun.

I'm wrong. There is something to be scared of.

I'm afraid of disappointing him.

I really have no business being in his bed. This level

of intimacy is something I left by the side of the road years ago. Ever since I aged out of foster care and started living on my own, autonomy has been my drug of choice. I have sex to scratch an itch, not to connect. Once you start connecting, you're screwed. I keep love at a distance. I don't give any more than what's required and I don't let anyone under my skin.

Until now, it's been quick, impersonal fucks. The less kissing, the better. I never take all my clothes off. Never lay down if I don't have to. I don't hang around afterward. I don't get emotional. I sure as hell don't get scared.

Lying here, naked as birth, my mouth swollen from kissing, my belly quivering under Chen's fingertips...I'm terrified.

I *do not* let people fuck me.

I don't let people close to me, let alone *into* me.

Except Chen. Fucking Chen who would never hurt anyone or anything. Chen who feels guilty for swatting a mosquito. Chen, who is the most dangerous kind of partner for me because he doesn't carelessly screw. He doesn't know how. He's always involved. Unapologetically emotional. Fearlessly afraid.

He's looking at me now. Waiting.

He wants to make love and I don't know how.

"I think I'm gonna remember this forever," he says.

I hold one corner of my bottom lip with my teeth and mumble out the other side, "You want me to turn over?"

His expression goes from magic to alarm, eyebrows

knitting. "Do you want to? I mean... Whatever's easiest for you."

His heat burns my eyes. "It's easiest if you just tell me what to do the first time."

He pitches forward, a hand on either side of my shoulders, his hair swooping down and I reach to brush it back. "Stay relaxed for me, okay? And trust me. That's all I want you to do."

He kisses me and I wrap my arms hard around his body, pulling him down. I need all his weight on me. Crushing just to the point where it's an effort to breathe. Same way a weighted blanket breaks apart my anxiety, Chen's weight is grounding. It fills every inch of my arms. It's like holding a big armful of towels that just came out of the dryer. I can feel his cock, hard on the inside of my leg, sliding up and then rubbing along my erection. His hands slide down my sides, down my legs and they hook under my knees. He brings them up around his hips and settles a little more on me, sliding and rubbing. Working his way down to line up the head with my hole. He presses a little and I tense up and clench. I can't help it. I trust him but I'm just so fucking *nervous*.

"It's okay," he says against my neck. He takes another pump of lube, then reaches down between us to slick up and position himself a little better. I just breathe and concentrate on staying relaxed and staying open. I'm expecting it to hurt. I just don't want it to *suck*.

He's pushing into me and it seems impossible. I know it can be done but my body thinks I'm crazy.

"Easy," he says softly, then leans down and kisses me. "I got you."

He kisses me again, opening a thick flush in my chest and throat. It spreads through my body, flooding every nerve and cell. My next inhale is almost a snarl and I let my teeth drag along his tongue. I want him bad and Chen must feel it, because he rocks back and pushes one of my knees up a little more. Then all at once, with a short, slippery thrust, the tip of his cock is inside me.

"*God,*" he whispers.

Everything stops dead. The night hangs frozen in the air, fixed in fire, not ice. A burning ball of hot, dry suspension and I'm in the middle.

"Breathe," he says. He threads all ten of his fingers with all ten of mine. "Breathe with me. Let everything go."

I can't breathe. I can barely get my mind wrapped around what's happening while my body just stares, wide-eyed and gaping. Chen's in me and it is *tight.* It's *intense.* It burns and stretches and I can feel my pulse hammering in my ass, beating around that fullness. He is *in* me.

"Fuck," I whisper slowly, yellow specks dancing in front of my eyes.

"Hurt?"

My voice sounds far away. "A little. It's all right." I breathe out slow and the pain lengthens. But it also gets thinner. The stretch of a tight muscle that howls but it still feels good to push a little deeper and sink into it.

I think the trick is not to be afraid of it.

"Too much?" Chen's looking at me a little sideways, eyes fierce. "I'll stop whenever you want."

"No, I'm okay."

He lets go my hands, puts his weight on one arm and the other palm runs over my forehead and through my hair. "You sure? I need you to tell me."

"Yeah. Is it..." I swallow. "Is it good?"

"Oh Christ, you have no idea." His laughing face is fucking beautiful. "God, you idiot."

Laughter hiccups in my chest. "Well, I need *you* to tell me, too."

"I can't tell you how good it feels."

"Yeah?"

"Jesus, yes. I can't believe this is happening."

Everything below my ribs, which felt like one giant clenched fist, eases up a little and I can get a deep breath into my lungs. "Let me feel you move," I say. "Go slow."

He backs out a bit, squeezes some lube on us then moves into me again. It's so fucking full and so fucking weird. But when Chen wraps his slippery hand around my cock and starts to squeeze in time with that little two-inch thrust in and out, it feels so fucking good.

"Good?" he says.

A lot of incoherent babbling starts to come out of my mouth, sandwiched between laughing gasps and garbled groans. Chen's laughing softly over me. "God, you're beautiful." His mouth comes down and covers mine and I suck on his tongue while he strokes and jerks and slides.

Soon all the screaming in my head condenses down to one word, which I push behind Chen's teeth over and over.

"More."

His thrusts don't speed up but they start to go longer. And deeper. Until he's not just in my ass but he is *up* my ass. A little bit more each time and then all the way out, holding me open at the peak. I groan every time he holds it there and I start to tilt up to meet his hips now. My hands pull him in and he sinks down on both elbows, letting his stomach slide over my cock and putting his heart on mine.

"Hold still," he says.

"You okay?"

"Yeah. Feel me right there?"

"Yeah?"

"I can't go any further. You took all of me."

"I can't believe this."

"Me neither."

"It feels okay?"

"It feels more than okay. This is so far beyond okay. It's a totally different universe."

I get one hand in his hair and the other spread wide on his jaw and I kiss hell out of him. Our teeth clatter and it's like we're trying to eat each other alive.

"I want you to come," I say against Chen's mouth. "Don't hold back, okay? I'd rather this were too short than too long."

"You need me to stop now?"

"No, I'm good."

"Don't lie to me. Please. I don't want to hurt you."

"I swear I'm good right now. But I won't be able to go much longer. Come now. I want you to come. You waited so long for this, man. Just take it. Put it in me."

"You don't know." His voice is hoarse. "You don't know how long I... You don't know what I wanted all these..." He breaks off, shaking his head. "You don't know."

"Show me."

Something in him seems to rev like an engine. The breath in his throat solidifies into a groan as the sweat rises to the surface of his skin.

"Tell me," I say, tightening my hand in his hair. "Tell me what it's been like all these years."

"Wanted you so bad," he says. "Not just this. Everything. Wanted to be with you. All the time. So bad it hurt. Like my heart would hurt. My head and my bones."

"Say more."

"I can't believe you came to me. I can't believe you're letting me do this."

"This?"

He holds still, buried balls-deep in me, pulsing and burning. "All my daydreams, all my stupid fantasies. Never once did I imagine you'd let me top you. Never."

"Did you want to?"

"I *wanted* it. But..." His smile unfolds and he starts to move again, real slow. "To get it to work in my mind, I had to let you top."

"To work in your mind?"

"Oh God, man. You don't know how long I've been making myself come, thinking about you."

"Show me."

That revving engine roars. It paws at the ground like a bull about to charge. Chen moves a little faster than before. Eyes closed and mouth a little open. He's waited years for this.

Years for this.

"It's so good," he whispers. "You feel so fucking good."

He sounds almost choked up. His voice is this vulnerable fragile thread coming out of his big body. Squeezing past all the hard, tight muscles in his chest and arms and shoulders. Tiny in his mouth like speaking it out loud will make it disappear. Make *me* disappear.

Me.

He could have anyone.

He wants lost, angry, fucked-up me.

I look up at him, hook my heel around the back of his leg and tug him in tighter. Filling myself up with his body and filling my eyes with his face.

"God," he whispers.

"I love this," I say. It feels braver than saying I love you. I always loved him. But *this*... I didn't think it could ever be mine.

"Feel good?" he says, working his hips into me.

"I love it." I open everything wide, letting him in.

"Chen, I love it."

He cries out, fingers curling into the sheets by my head. His back tenses and the muscles in his jaw flicker. He holds back even as he's letting go, careful not to buck too hard as he comes into me and doesn't stop.

It's fucking beautiful. His weight fills my arms again as he writhes over the crest of the wave and comes to a stop. A little edge of teeth against my shoulder and a bite of his fingernails in my back. Slowly he grows still. I lay my hand on his sweaty head, holding it against my heartbeat.

A long moment in the dark where I want for nothing. And I wonder if maybe Chen is asleep but then he stirs and pushes up on his hands.

"All right?" he says, carefully moving out of me. I wince, biting my lip. It hurts more to stop than to be doing it.

"Now I'm sore."

"It'll calm down in a minute," he says, chucking the condom.

He makes me take two Tylenol and lie on my stomach with a cold washcloth pressed into my crack.

"Water's dripping off my balls now," I say.

"I'll sleep in the wet spot."

"Gee, thanks."

He presses his mouth into the cap of my shoulder and his hand moves in long strokes up and down my back. "I'd do anything for you."

"Yeah?"

"After tonight? I'm fucking yours."

I close my eyes. My body is sore and tired like I just got back from the gym. I didn't even come and I'm still full of endorphin-drenched euphoria.

Maybe that's what making love does to you.

Chen pulls me toward him, his hand running through my hair. "That was so good."

"Liar."

"I'm not lying. It was amazing."

My face gets all hot. Fucking Chen and the way he can make me blush, I swear to God.

"What?" he says, teeth shining in his smile.

"Nothing." The washcloth's gone lukewarm now. I reach back and toss it away, then roll to my back.

"All right?"

"All right." I open my arms. "Come here, stupid."

Laughing, Chen puts his head on my chest. I fold my arms around his shoulders. I love how he fits into me. Love how his thick hair fills my hand. Love the hot, dry smell of his skin.

"I'll definitely remember this forever," he says, drawing circles around my belly button.

"You better."

I never sleep well without my weighted blanket but tonight, under nothing but a thin sheet and Chen's head, I fall asleep fast. Concrete, dreamless sleep. I wake up to Chen kissing down my chest and stomach, closing his big hand around my hardening cock. I go from zombie to lunatic in six seconds, pushing aside the covers and spreading my legs, letting him get down on me.

"I'm gonna make you come into next week," he says, and then he sucks me down so fast and deep, I lose my mind. My back bows up like I'm being shocked and I'm crying his name through my teeth. His mouth. God, his mouth. It's the one thing in the entire universe right now. This right here, right now and nothing else but Chen fucking me with his mouth.

"Baby," I whisper. I've never called anyone baby in my life but it slips easy out of my mouth and floats over the bed.

He nudges my calf up on his shoulder, then his hand glides between my legs and up my back. He leaves my hole alone, just keeps a steady warm pressure next to the fevered rhythm of his mouth. But I'm thinking about his cock now. Remembering that hot fullness inside me and thinking I can take it again. Realizing I want it again. I want *this* again.

God, I'm fucked. For real. It's my turn. Chen hit my reset button and my years start over tonight. It'll be me now, thinking about Chen, going crazy with wanting and longing. Hurting to my heart and bones. Getting myself off to memories of this night and daydreams of doing it again. Wondering when it will be again. When, *when* will we do this again?

My fingers fist into his hair and I come and come in his mouth until I feel close to dead. He groans around my cock, a keening sound like he's coming with me. I collapse cursing back into the covers, my chest heaving and sucking wind. Chen's sprawled out with his face on my hip, breathing just as hard, damp and choppy across my stomach. He reaches up and I reach down. Our hands clasp and hold on tight.

"Man, I can't believe this," he says.

Tears sting the back of my eyes as I start counting the seconds.

LOVE WAS AN UNDERSTATEMENT

THE SKIES WERE DOVE-GREY and thick with clouds when they returned to the house, hands full of local treasure: two bottles of Eastern Cove Cygnet from the Florance vineyard, a jar of the island's famed Ligurian honey, and four southern rock lobsters caught just hours ago. These had been carefully prepped for transport by the mongers, lovingly placed in a Styrofoam cooler lined with layers of damp newspapers and seaweed.

"Put it straight in the fridge, loves," they were advised, and sure enough, on the north side of the house was a large outdoor refrigerator Joe and Jean had installed specifically for the storing of live lobsters.

"You're coming?" Jean had squealed last week when they had phoned from Adelaide. "When? Oh dammit, we're going to Tassie for a wedding. Too bad. Oh well, take the house anyway. Don't be ridiculous, take it, you can look after the dogs and that saves us the hassle of boarding them. Win-win. We'll leave you the key. You'll love it."

Love was an understatement. They were smitten the instant they walked through the door and they exhausted their curse words as they wandered from room to room. Taking in the view of the ocean from every window, the open floor plan, the soaring ceilings, the air and light and space and utter perfection of this beach house, right down to the two sober border collies in their care for the next four days.

Lobsters safely stowed, they flung the rest of their loot on the kitchen table. It was four o'clock, not quite dinnertime. Katherine wanted to nap. Will said he wasn't tired, he'd take the dogs for a walk. So in one of their rare instances, they parted ways, she upstairs to the bedroom, he out the back deck and down to the sand, the collies following close on his heels.

Like a femme fatale, she pushed back the thin, voile drapes of the bedroom window and watched him stride over the dunes, hands in the pockets of the grey drawstring pants he seemed to live in these days, rolled up around his calves. The temperature had dropped and he'd pulled on a blue chambray shirt. It flapped around and behind him like a sail.

Out of the house ten seconds and she missed him.

Her fingertips traced the window, touching his far-away image, keeping it in sight. She watched him walk along, kick at the ground with his bare feet, bend to pick things up. Some he flung ahead, a few he put in his pocket. Maybe he'd found her a shell. He was always bringing her little things from the beach and she had a collection of them on her bedside table. Shells and pebbles and sea glass and feathers.

He stopped and sat down on the sand. One of the dogs lay in a dark heap beside him, the other continued to romp around down by the waves. He was too far for such details, but she pretended anyway she could see how the wind was catching his hair, how one or two tiny grains of sand might have caught in his eyebrows, how his face settled into that smooth, expansive expression that meant he was thinking intently of something, or not thinking at all.

She toyed briefly with the idea of grabbing a shawl and walking out after him, but she was chilled off now, as well as sleepy, and the bed beckoned with soft sheets and blankets. She let the drapes fall and crawled in, pulled the covers nearly over her head and tucked her cool hands under her chin. He'd be back soon. And with that, the edges of her mind dissolved away rapidly.

She slept hard, dreamlessly, slowly came back to now, up through levels of consciousness, forgetting where she was, then remembering. Will's head dipped below her chin, covering her neck with long, lingering kisses. She sighed with him, her hands roaming. His hair smelled like wind and sea. His shirt was a little damp.

"Did you have a good walk?" she said, eyes still closed.

"No, not really."

"No?"

He had pulled the sheet over their heads, making a

dark, secret cave. His hands were cold and he crept them along the back of her head, digging his fingers into the warmth of her hair. She moved closer to him and he kissed her softly.

"Why?" she said again, and began undoing the buttons on his shirt.

His fingers spread wide to cradle her head and his mouth closed gently on her bottom lip, then let it go. "Too many years," he said between kisses. "There were too many years without you. And now... I don't like not being around you. Any time I go away, or do something without you, I only want to come back and tell you about it. Maybe someday I'll get into solitude again but right now...I just want to be with you."

He pulled his arms free of the sleeves, tossed the shirt onto the floor, then pulled her own T-shirt over her arms, slid her skirt and underwear off and threw them away as well. She took his head, kissed his lips apart and tasted him. She didn't like to think about the lost years, didn't like to think of time in general where they were concerned. They had the luxury of being able to ignore time, throw it away. No past regrets. No future plans. Only now. Only here. Only him.

"I just want you," he said. His skin to hers, she could feel the heat rising in him and her own body rising up to meet it. He rolled onto her and they kissed, then he rolled on his back and pulled her on his chest and they kissed more, her hair falling around their heads. Back and forth like the ocean waves they rolled across the bed, and then settled down on their sides once more, curled into each other, tangled like vines, kissing deep.

"I'm so hard for you," he said softly. She reached down, pulled his drawstring and closed him up in her hand, helped him kick the pants away. Fresh desire settled thickly in her chest, along with the damp ache of wanting to feel him in her again. Again, again, they were making love all the time and it was never enough. She rolled and put her back to his chest, pushing her butt up against his lap, guiding him into her.

"Slow, put it in me slow," she whispered.

Inch by inch he took her, her hipbones snugged in his palms. Then he wrapped his arms around her waist, covering her back with all his body, and groaned into her hair, "God you make me crazy."

She was beside herself with pure, primal want. He rolled up on his knees, bringing her with him. She reached and flung her arms around his neck, loving the feel of him against her back, he was so strong. They kissed deep, mouths soft, slippery and reckless. His hand slid down between her legs. He ran his lips over her back, whispered to her, encouraged and cajoled her, bringing her around with a skilled ease that made her think, not for the first time, that he was born to love her.

She cried a little, she couldn't help it. "Too many years," she joked weakly, trying to hide her face but he wouldn't let her. So unbearably sweet to her, he held her head, made her face him, and gently kissed the wet trails on her face.

"It's all right," he whispered, before he enveloped her in his arms and pulled her against his chest. She could feel his heart pounding against hers. His mouth was so tender on her forehead, she thought she might die.

"This," she whispered. "This. It's all I want."

"This," he echoed. "I've waited years for this..."

Our Place

Zermatt
Switzerland

OUTSIDE, SNOWFLAKES LARGE AS LEAVES were piling in drifts on their balcony. Inside, the fire was mellowing to embers behind the brass grate. They had made love and now lay in each other's arms, naked under piles of covers, not sleepy, but just content in the dim, magic hours of midnight. The cuckoo clock chimed a quarter-hour, which never failed to make them smile.

"We need to get one of those," he said. "Put it in our bedroom so I can always remember this night."

"Remember the first time we made love?" she asked.

"I remember every time we made love."

"You do not."

"I do. Most of them, anyway. Definitely the first time, though."

She raised up on an elbow, the other hand moving in slow circles on his torso, making him want to purr. "You were nineteen," she said thoughtfully.

He chuckled. "I couldn't believe it. You were such a woman."

"I was a kid."

"Not to me. You were... I mean, you were just out of my league. It was crazy. I couldn't believe this gorgeous grad student wanted me."

She eased over to lay on him, crossing her forearms on his chest and resting her chin atop. She was tousled and still a little sweaty and completely adorable. "I remember how you looked under me. Like when I was pushing you back to lie down so I could get on top of you. You were shaking."

"I was overwhelmed. I told you, you were the most beautiful girl I'd even seen. And it was just a dream for me."

"Tell me more."

"About what? That night?"

"Whatever you remember. Close your eyes. Think back and take me there."

He knew she wanted a story, and it would have been easy to protest that he couldn't remember enough of the details. But for her, he would try. He closed his eyes, let his body rest and sink into the mattress, let her warm weight press on him, press him back through the years. He put his hand into her damp hair. Always her hair anchored him to the past, to those early heady days of love. He wound it around his fingers, reached for something. A sense memory.

"You had that hair gel that smelled like grape candy," he said slowly.

"Me and every other girl on earth."

"It was March, right? No. February. Valentine's Day?"

"The day before, actually."

"I think I was trying to wait until Valentine's Day but then…I couldn't."

"Everyone else has Valentine's Day. We have Valentine's Eve."

"We were in your room," he said. He kept his eyes shut and let his mind drift, reach back, gather up the memories. He let himself talk, ramble, sketch it out for her, and he was astonished at how easily it came back to him…

* * * * *

SHE WAS BUSY WITH WRITING or some involved project at her desk, her head bent over her work and the lamplight picking up the red bits in her dark hair. He was reading *Rolling Stone*, perfectly comfortable in her silence, yet he kept looking up from his magazine. Something about the room kept drawing off his attention. Something was important here.

He looked around. The room was larger than most dorm rooms. More spacious because only one person was occupying it, with the added luxury of an adjoining bathroom. He gazed at the furnishings and decorations he'd been looking at for nine weeks now. The little coffee machine, her tape deck, the brass baker's rack where her clothes were stacked. He began to notice his own possessions among hers. His cap was on the dresser by the bathroom door. His coat hung in the closet. His shoes on the floor, his wallet and keys on the desk.

His gaze passed by the open bathroom door again, then stopped and backtracked. Focusing through the doorway to the sink. His toothbrush in the rack next to hers.

He had a toothbrush here. That was her doing, not his. They weren't sleeping together, not yet. But he had been sleeping over quite a while, and at one point she had simply bought him a toothbrush. There it was. In her bathroom. In her room. Which, tonight, felt very much like *their* room.

He tried that on. *Our room.*

He went a step further. *Our place.*

This meager ten-by-ten space where he could set down his bits and pieces and have a toothbrush in the bathroom. A place with a door they could shut and seal themselves off from the world.

Then the concept that had been tantalizingly evading him all night revealed itself, and the concept was *privacy*. Private moments were few and far between at college. The point of college was socialization, you had to make a concerted effort to get away from people, even the sound of their voices was a constant background hum everywhere you went.

Tonight, here, it was quiet and peaceful within the walls of her room. Just them. No interruptions. No one and nothing else, nowhere to go.

"What are you thinking about?" Her voice floated into

his thoughts. She was looking over at him, soft and rumpled in her sweats and T-shirt, her long hair spilling over her shoulders, her upper lip curling into that smile he loved.

I love her. It was part of this room. Built into the floors and ceilings, the concrete and linoleum. He was here. He was six weeks shy of his twentieth birthday and he was in love.

He glanced at the clock on her desk, the clock that woke the both of them most mornings. "It's after one," he said. A Tuesday night was now the wee hours of Wednesday morning. He didn't have to leave. No curfew to keep, no rules to obey, no parents to answer to. He could stay. He was allowed here. He belonged here.

Our place.

He put aside his magazine and swung his feet to the floor. Reaching for the arms of her chair, he turned her in it to face him, and then slid off the bed so he was kneeling between her feet. She looked at him and he looked back, ensnared in her gaze, unable to look away, harboring no desire to. His hands slid along the sides of her face, fingertips in the hair over her ears. Not closing his eyes, he found her mouth with his, kissing her softly once, then again, once more, nudging her lips apart so he could feel her breathe into him.

Her knees pressed against the outsides of his legs, her hands glided up his arms. His own hands moved, down her shoulders and arms, the feel of her warm skin under clothes, the lift of her chest as she arched into his hands holding her breasts now, her mouth opening, the slide of her tongue on his, the grape-candy smell of her hair.

He pulled her off the chair into his lap, tucked her good into one elbow and kissed her, the other hand stroking her hair, her neck, her breasts, sliding down her stomach. Across her sweats, cupping between her legs and holding that damp heat that he had created in her.

He stopped kissing and held her tight to his chest, staring in her eyes. Something deep within him began to tremble. "I love you," he whispered in her mouth.

"I love you."

"I'm so in love with you." The trembling intensified.

She kissed him again, held his head in her hands, turned it this way and that as she kissed his mouth, staring in his eyes. He wanted to fall into those eyes forever, fall clear into her body and be inside everything he loved about her. Nine weeks. He was done waiting. He was sure.

"I'm ready if you are," he said softly.

She, five weeks shy of her twenty-second birthday, could have teased him. But she didn't. Her own limbs were shaking now, and she drew in a deep breath and let it go slowly.

"You sure?" she whispered.

He nodded, his forehead to hers. "Positive."

"You love me?"

"Yes."

"You want to be inside me?"

"Yes." He groaned it, catching her mouth up in his

again, desire coursing like a flooded river through his young body, coiled tight with heat and longing, yearning to coil up with hers.

She got up from his lap, stood up and turned off the lamp, plunging the room into darkness. Only a small slice of yellow-orange streetlight came through a gap in the curtains. She held her hands out to him, he took them, and she brought him to his feet and started undoing the buttons on his shirt.

* * * * *

"SHAKING," HE SAID NOW, years later, in a hotel room in Switzerland with that girl, now this woman, lying on him, silhouetted in firelight. "Getting out of our clothes. Shaking. Kissing, rolling around, touching, shaking. You putting the condom on me. Shaking. You were so confident. You just got on top of me and like *took* me and *put* me in you and it was the greatest fucking thing ever."

He drifted in the memory, parts of which remained vivid enough to make his toes curl. He was starting to get hard again, just remembering sliding into her body for the first time.

"We did it three times," she said.

"Well, the first time didn't last long. I couldn't handle you."

"The second was longer," she conceded. "And the third time..." She leaned and kissed him slowly. "Third time was magic."

He slid his hands into her hair. "Every time was magic," he said. "But that first time was a gift. I don't think you'll ever know what it meant to me."

He kissed her, momentarily captured in the emotional complexity of that evening, remembering he'd known without a shred of doubt that he was in love with this girl. That combined with the beauty of her body and how she had just put him on his back, got on him and guided him into her—it left him reeling. He hadn't been a virgin, but it had been like nothing he'd ever known. Not before. Not since.

"It meant the world to me," he said. "Being your lover changed me."

"I know," she said against his mouth. "Maybe I didn't know then but I know now."

Desire was closing over him like quicksand, dragging him down into syrupy longing. "I'm so hard for you," he said.

"I know."

"Put me in you. Like you did the first time."

She rose up over him, her thighs snugging up his sides. One of her hands on his shoulder, the other reaching for his cock, sliding along it, squeezing him, guiding the head to that pulsing heat. Letting it part her, open her. She let go of him, leaned on both his shoulders and he slid full into her, deep, deeper than he'd ever been. He wasn't shaking now. He was strong, on fire, burning bright, older now and able to handle it when she sent him reeling.

"You move in me like you were born to," she whispered.

"I was born to." He took her hands, looked up at her, looked up into the past as she stared back down at him from the present. "I was made for this."

The embers of the fire smoldered, the snow piled up against the windows, the cuckoo chimed another quarter hour.

SHE KNEW KILLARNEY WELL

SHE TOOK HER TEA OUTSIDE to look at the view while he called ahead to the hotel in Killarney and confirmed their reservation. The bargirl chatted him up a while. She was from Tralee but she knew Killarney well, and recommended a small restaurant for dinner where the fish was superb. Lovely grass-fed beef or lamb on the menu, too, if he didn't care for fish. He thanked her and headed outside.

The lake water was an astonishing turquoise, lapping up to a bone-white beach. Looking only at the water, one would think they were in Bermuda, but then rising straight up from its smooth expanse were those vertical cliffs, domed with emerald grass, and beyond them the water took on a more royal blue tone. The wind was clear and cold and the sun cast handfuls of diamonds along the lake surface.

She had found a bench on the bluff, and was perched on the back of it, her feet on the seat. She sat, still and pretty in her grey coat with her hands warmed around the cup on her knees, gazing out at the lake through her sunglasses, the wind intermittently lifting her hair up and off her shoulders. Something nudged his memory. He stopped, looked at her curiously, walked a few more steps, then stopped again, his breath stilled. He had seen this before.

He had been breathless that day, nothing but a pounding heart and stomach as he drove his car into the parking lot. She was waiting for him, waiting right where she said she would be, sitting on the trunk of her car. She had been wearing the grey coat and her sunglasses. Holding a cup between her hands. She smiled as he pulled up and parked. He tried to not explode out of the car and run to her, but he came around at a brisk walk, his heart swelling until he was nothing but a heart. A heart on shaking legs.

She sat with her feet together on the bumper and her gloved hands in her lap, holding her cup, smiling at him, the wind blowing her hair. His girl.

He said something clever as he came closer, he couldn't remember now. She said something just as clever in reply and set down her cup. Then in one fluid, rippling motion she planted her feet on the bumper and rose up. As her coat fell open, he caught a glance of a black sweater and her long legs in jeans flexing, straightening. She jumped. She *dove* at him, leaped the space between them and landed in his arms.

He made some kind of sound when her weight smacked his chest, something between a gasp and a moan, maybe the beginnings of a sob. Like springs his arms snapped shut around her and he heaved her up against him, with the distinct possibility of toppling over backward on the pavement but he didn't give a damn. He wasn't letting go, not now, not ever, never again.

Her face to his, she clutched at his shoulders. For an instant he felt her calves on his hips: she nearly got her legs around him too, which would have wrecked him. She put her feet down, counterbalancing, pulling them back until she was up against her car and there they clung to each other. Wrapping and re-wrapping their arms, over, under, here, there, trying to get closer. First she tore off her gloves and threw them carelessly on the ground so her hands could feel his head. Then she flung her sunglasses aside to better burrow into his chest. He took her head, tilted her face up in the sunshine. His girl. Now this woman. He kissed her hair, her forehead, her cheeks, her nose, her chin, her jaw. He held her in his hands and gently put his mouth on hers, just once, and her lips were soft and she pulled her breath in through her nose.

Face to face, breathing each other, his hands parted the lapels of her coat like curtains and slid around her waist. He slid across the softness of her sweater, feeling muscle and bone beneath. Feeling how her body had changed but not the electric thrill of it, if anything that was stronger. The time to be polite had passed. It was too late to pretend, too late to avoid. He had looked for her and she was there. They were there. *It* was there, ready to be found. She was in his arms now, her breath was his breath and he was hungry, so hungry. He tugged at her sweater where it was tucked into her jeans, pulled it free. As his hands glided over the skin of her back for the first time in over ten years, a surge of raw emotion hit him in the knees. He began to shake and could not stop.

On the shore of an Irish lake now, he looked at her. His girl, waiting for him. Right where she said she would be.

He started walking again, stopped just in front of her.

"It's so beautiful," she said, her profile clear and clean against the turquoise waters.

"Do you know what you look like?" he said softly. "Right now?"

Her head tilted to him, then she looked down at herself. Three beats of silence and she smiled at her lap. She knew.

She set aside her cup, planted her feet down on the bench seat and jumped. She leaped the space between them, into his arms, which were waiting.

SPELLBOUND

Jason met Milan Lenda at a bar called Willow Street. A band called the Authority was playing, fronted by an intense, River Phoenix lookalike. The guitarist looked in perpetual agony. The bass player was definitely one of the FBI's Most Wanted. They tried a little too hard with the smoke machine and ultraviolet light scheme, but in between the techno-angst originals, they got over themselves and played some decent covers of U2 and the Police.

Jason was a stranger here, having come up from Philadelphia to visit his cousin in Port Chester. Lou had already wandered off after a chick, leaving Jason sitting on a wide ledge that ran around the perimeter of the open space, not knowing a soul and used to barhopping in groups. He embraced the invisible solitude, passed silent judgment of the band and people-watched, trying to guess who was getting laid with whom tonight.

It took all of ten minutes to notice two women close by. Then five more seconds for his gaze to squeeze tight on the brunette.

She stood with her back to him, dancing in place. Feet rooted to the ground and pure liquid from the ankles up. Subtle, but uninhibited, with a syncopated rhythm in her torso that nailed all the accents of the percussion section. He liked how the tumble of dark hair between her shoulder blades moved in counterpoint to her shoulders. He liked that she was sweating, and how the part of her back not obscured by her hair glistened. And he liked that she wasn't dancing and trying to scope the scene at the same time. Her eyes never left the stage. She was there for the music.

He liked her on sight. She looked good from behind, a thought that got his own back sweating. The song ended and she gathered her hair in a fist and waved the back of her damp neck with it. Then she tucked her beer bottle in the crook of one elbow, and with her free hand began pulling a wad of cash from the hip pocket of her jeans.

Jason slid off the ledge, walked toward her and asked over her left shoulder: "What are you going to do with all that money?"

She gave him a glance and what stuck in his mind forever after, was how unsurprised that glance was. How accepting of his sudden presence and how immediately familiar her tone of voice, as if they'd grown up down the street from one another, been part of the same circle of friends, and had come together to the bar tonight.

She said, "Here, hold this," thrusting her beer into his hand. Her chin stretched left and right, looking around.

"Where'd Jen go?"

"That way, I think." He assumed Jen was her friend. Again the familiarity, as if he already knew all her pals' names. "What's with the cash?"

"I wanted to see if I had enough money to buy their demo CD and still drink."

"Go get the demo," he said, wobbling the empty bottle in his hand. "I'll take care of this."

That was it. They met as if picking up from a conversation that got interrupted in a previous life, each one's ear perfectly suited to the other's voice.

They didn't see each other for five months after the night at Willow Street, only talked on the phone. They called while driving, making dinner and watching TV. They called first thing in the morning, or last thing at night, or talked all night and fell asleep with the line still open. They told weird life stories, admitted vices, divulged secrets and made ugly confessions.

And they masturbated a ton.

"I can't have phone sex with anybody but you," Jason said. "With anybody else, it's ridiculous. I mean *I* feel ridiculous. And phony."

"Same," she said. "It's amazing with you. It's both genuine and surreal. I mean, half the time I don't even know who I am when I'm fucking you on the phone."

"Right? Jesus, sometimes I can't believe the shit that comes out of my mouth."

In reply came the distinctive sound of her inhaling and exhaling. Like an ocean wave drowning him in salty slow-motion, making his eyes fall closed and sending a hand straight down his pants.

They never tried to fall in love. Their differences were far too myriad. Sometimes they talked on the phone every night for a week. Sometimes weeks passed with no contact. But whenever the connection was remade, it always began with the same immediate, mid-sentence affinity—*So anyway, like I was saying*—and usually ended in orgasm, followed by a long, slow, sleepy goodnight.

They took perverse pleasure in listing all the ways they'd make a terrible couple. But they could talk like there was no tomorrow and fuck like nobody's business. Which was why, a year and change after meeting—an interval measured in a dozen hotel rooms, a thousand long-distance phone calls and a flood of magnificent sex—Milan arrived at Jason's apartment at eleven o'clock on a Tuesday night. Burst through in belted trench coat and heels, slammed the door and fell back against it with an abrupt exhale, as if having just escaped the Gestapo.

"You made it," Jason said.

"Not yet."

She tilted her face up and he kissed her mouth. Already the spicy, orange-and-clove smell of her perfume was in his nose and mouth, filling his head and tickling the back of his throat. The scent was called Spellbound and it was permanently linked to Milan in his mind. It could stop him in his tracks and make him glance around for her. He'd wandered after it in department stores more than once. A woman he took out to dinner wore

Spellbound and when he fucked her later, he thought of Milan and didn't even feel bad about it.

"What's under this?" he asked, tugging at her lapels.

"You'll see," she said primly, ducking under his arm and walking through the sliding doors that led to his bedroom. He caught her elbow and with the other hand, brushed her hair off the back of her neck and put his mouth there. A rash of goose bumps rippled across her skin and she leaned back on his chest. He could feel her body underneath her coat, easily inferring it wasn't clothed in much.

"You smell good," he said, licking where the fine baby hairs made a V on her nape.

"Mm." She was untying the belt and undoing buttons. Underneath the coat she wore the mother of all Victoria's secrets. A cliché getup of black lace and fishnets and skin peeking between straps and like a tired punchline, Jason was hard for it.

"You drove here wearing this?" he said.

"I did," she said. "I even stopped to get gas. On the New York side of the bridge, so I'd have to pump my own."

"You're insane."

"That wasn't enough of a thrill, so I went inside to get snacks. Gawky teenager at the register. If he only knew."

"Jesus."

"It was a weird thrill. But addicting. Before I got back on the Turnpike, I ditched the coat. Literally drove the rest of the way here in my underwear."

"What if you got pulled over?"

"That was the thrill of it." She kissed his mouth. "You like?"

"It's nice," he whispered as she let her coat drop off her shoulders. It fell in a puddle around their feet.

"Just nice?"

"It's tremendous," he said, running his hands down her back, feeling the goose bumps come and go.

"It's not very practical. I'm not sure how it all comes off."

"Oh, it'll come off..." He wasn't sure himself. He'd get a pair of scissors and cut her out of it if he had to, but for the moment he took her by the shoulders and surveyed the full effect. "Walk around."

"Walk around?"

He sat down on the bed. "I want to look at you."

"I could make you a sandwich..." She stepped over the pile of her coat and strutted through the kitchen door. "Ham or turkey?"

"Get. Back. In. Here."

She walked through the bedroom and out to the living room, where she turned off the light.

"Now I can't see you," he said, then realized the bright moonlight coming through the window suited the mood better. "Never mind. Leave it."

She leaned on the door jamb, a hand on her hip. "You like?"

"I like."

"Good." She climbed up to sit on his desk, perched

on the edge with her feet planted on the seat of the chair. "Think you'd be able to study with me right here?" She leaned back and crossed her legs.

"I'd fail out."

"Oh. I'm not sitting on anything important here, am I? Legal briefs? Term paper?"

"You're sitting on my phone bill."

"How appropriate."

"Take it off now," he said, stretching out on his side, leaning on an elbow.

"Which part?"

"All of it."

The bra was tossed in his direction but fell short. She unhooked the garter belt and took it and the stockings off in one piece. In another moment, she sat with her arms wrapped around her knees, twirling the leghole of the black panties around her finger.

A long electric stare.

"You should be studying," she said.

He sighed and got up. "Fine."

She moved her feet so he could sit down, then rested them on either side of his legs. He could smell her already. He swallowed hard, his tongue twitching, and ran his hands up her calves. She was breathing heavier, each exhale making a tiny hum in the back of her throat. A small, involuntary sound of pleasure that never failed to turn him on, whether it was coming to him over the phone or from six inches away. She made those little sighs and he got hard. She said "hello," and he got hard.

Now she sat naked on top of his desk, opening her knees to him. He didn't know how he'd ever be able to sit here and study again, but he wouldn't have swapped places with anyone for anything.

Her breasts filled his hands, the nipples hard like pearls between his fingers before softening in his mouth. The desire to taste her became less of a desire and more of a need and his hands moved in between her thighs. Slowly, carefully, he pried her open, like separating the petals of a rose, leaned forward and ran his tongue up and down the pale pink flesh. She collapsed back against the wall, upsetting a pile of books. He went deeper. Lost in her smell and taste and sound, making her come, and making her come, and making her come again, until there was no telling where her wetness stopped and his mouth began and he was moaning into her as loudly as she moaned into the air.

He was helpless. Milan had him spellbound. The beast in him was awake, ravenous and irrational, wanting to run fangs along her skin, snarl up her limbs and eat her alive.

Sorceress, he thought, up to his chin in her, looking for one word to pin down this hold she had on him.

Witch. Siren. Temptress.

Femme fatale.

Soulmate.

She defied description. Nobody made him lose his mind like Milan and nobody made him a more attentive, mindful lover. Nobody made him feel so helpless or so confident. So clueless and so skilled. Milan was *maddening* to him, yet sex with her was one of the simplest and purest things he knew.

Her last orgasm shivered on his tongue and he caught his breath, rubbing his mouth on the inside of her thigh while she gasped against her hands, "Take your clothes off."

He pulled off his T-shirt and scooted out of his football shorts just as she came sliding off the desk and onto his lap. She spit in her hand and closed it around the erection he'd been sporting since he called to invite, ask or beg this crazy lady over and she not only said yes, but drove here half-naked.

"So hard," she said between her teeth.

"Put it in you," he whispered, trying to pull her down. She slithered out of his clutching grip and between his thighs, down onto her knees. When she looked up at him, her eyes were bad in the moonlight.

"Not yet," she said. Then her hair filled his lap and her mouth was on him. Her tongue running up and down, circling the tip, sucking at him. Then she was holding him in her hands and swallowing him into the smoothest, darkest part of her throat. Breathing around him, warm and wet, then releasing him into the cool air. Drawing him back in and he could feel that tiny little moan vibrate around his cock.

His hands held her head, stroked her jaw and the back of her neck. He heard his voice far away. Moaning her name. A *Milan* that encouraged. A *Milan* that pleaded. The razor-sharp *Milan* that buffeted him along the thin tightrope between control and surrender.

"Milan, I swear to God..."

The beast grew greedier, more insatiable, until Jason would've sold his soul to have either three clones or four dicks, so he could come in Milan's mouth, in her hands, on her breasts and in her pussy all at the same time.

He was slumped down in the chair now, legs stretched long and head tipped back. One hand clutching the armrest, the other wrapped in her hair. Grunting, moaning and hissing as he canted his hips up to her mouth. Teetering on a precipice of wanting her so badly, it pissed him off. She made him feel so utterly alive that he wanted to *kill* her. Yet when he sat up, reached down to take her face and bring it to his mouth, his kiss was soft, slow and tender because he knew no other way to kiss her.

"Come here." He stood and pulled her up, both of them stumbling to their feet and over to his bed.

They were ferocious, but oddly quiet lovers. As if they were so verbally aggressive and descriptive on the phone, they had no need to speak when they made love face to face. Two mute charioteers, they passed the reins back and forth. First him, taking her legs over his arms and sliding into her. Watching her eyes squeeze and her mouth strain, while her arms twisted and twined over her head and her calves lay limp on his elbows. Then she rolled onto him, pinning his wrists to the mattress, dangling her breasts over his mouth like a young nymph offering bunches of grapes to a Roman god. Raising and lowering her hips on him, keeping him on the edge, guided by his terse whispers every so often to stop.

"Stop," he whispered. "Stop stop wait... Not yet... Hold still..."

She hovered motionless as he wrestled the beast down from the edge, made him heel and behave.

"Good?" she said, running a hand along his face.

He turned his mouth into her palm. "Too good."

When a little more blood came back to his brain, he wrapped arms around her body and rolled her off him, down onto her stomach so he could fuck her from behind. First pulling her to her knees and holding her waist, burying himself in her, as deep as he could, grinding against her and watching the muscles of her back and ass ripple with each thrust. Then easing her down, prone on her stomach so he could cover her body with his, hold still and let her squeeze him from inside.

Over and over, racing laps around their *circus maximus.* They tore each other up and turned each other inside out, kissing and touching and wallowing in one another's bodies, until riding the edge started to hurt, hurt so good. Milan rose up over him, letting go of him completely and arching back, bucking her hips down on him and rubbing against his fingers until he could feel her start to come. The tremors in her thighs and a rush of more wetness around his aching cock. He flung her to the night and jumped after her. The beast howled, the chariot horses screamed. Jason's eyes locked onto the dark of Milan's mouth, bound to her spell.

They collapsed, panting and sweaty, onto the empty mattress. Pillows, topsheet and covers lay strewn and dead on the floor, victims of the gladiators.

"Milan," Jason murmured, kissing her swollen mouth over and over.

M'lady.

Mate.

He leaned, grabbed the nearest corner of the crumpled duvet and dragged it over them. Their breathing quieted, the kissing grew slower and softer, until they were yawning against each other's faces.

"You gonna stay?" he finally asked.

She flopped her arm across his damp chest, kissed his shoulder. "Have to," she said through a yawn. "I don't have anything to wear home."

TALKING TO STRANGERS

Eleven o'clock on a Tuesday night typically saw Jude in bed or heading toward it. Instead, he was in a booth at a Capitol Hill pub, heading toward his fourth beer.

I'm not my parents' child.

He'd never again use the word "stunned" lightly. He couldn't feel his face and he was sure the alcohol had nothing to do with it. One billion and seven thoughts careened through his brain, like an eclipse of moths around a lightbulb. *What the fuck* alighted on his shoulder, then flew off again. *I can't believe it* made loop-the-loops around his head, followed by a more sluggish *What do I do?*

What now?

Where do I go now?

He stared at the window. Sometimes through it, looking for answers on the street. Sometimes into it, catching his reflection in the window, unable to recognize his own face.

I'm not theirs.

So who am I?

What is my name?

"He's not worth it."

Startled, Jude looked the other way to see a man lounging against the booth. "What?"

"He shit on you. He broke your heart. Fuck it, things happen for a reason. He's not the one. This is happening because you're destined to meet someone better. I'm telling you, one day, you'll be lying in bed with the most excellent dude to walk the planet, and you'll look back on this night and wonder who that prophetic stranger at the bar was. I'll say you're welcome now."

Jude blinked. The guy kept smiling back, handsome and confident. A little too much of each, frankly. In Jude's experience, exceptionally good-looking men were either guarded as hell or entitled as hell, and this grinning tomcat exuded the latter.

"Do I know you?" Jude said.

"In the biblical sense? Not yet."

Jude stared, the hoppy air of the pub cool against his teeth and tongue.

"Close your mouth. It's making me have inappropriate thoughts."

Resisting the urge to check over his shoulder or point a finger at his chest, Jude said, "Are you hitting on me?"

"Are you available to be hit on?"

The sober Jude would roll his eyes and flick this lothario off like a horsefly. Instead he leaned back on the alcoholic buzz and settled into his skin. Gaze holding still as he took a long sip of his beer.

"Don't lick your lips like that," the lothario said. "It's not helping get rid of me."

Not looking away, Jude licked his lips again. The guy's head tipped back with laughter, showing a rather lovely throat.

"You got game," he said, sliding uninvited into the opposite bench. "I knew you did."

"What's your name?" Jude asked. Since when were throats a lovely thing to him? This one looked meaty rising up out of a shirt collar, with a bristle of incoming beard through the soft skin. Delectable little adam's apple rising and falling as he said, "I'm Tage."

Jude frowned. "Tage?"

"T-e-j. Rhymes with page."

"Tej. Cool name. I like it."

A long staring moment before Tej raised an eyebrow. "See, this is where you tell me your name."

"I'm sorry."

"Your name is sorry?"

"My name is Juleón. Friends call me Jude."

He'd punch this guy out if he started singing the Beatles.

"Nice to meet you, Juleón," Tej said. "So what's going on?"

"How old are you?"

Tej winced. "Dude, seriously?"

"I'm thirty-six and just found out I'm adopted."

"Now I'm losing my erection."

A waitress materialized and collected Jude's empty

glass. "Another one?"

"Please."

"Something for you, Tej?"

"I'll have what he's having. To soothe my wounded ego."

When she'd gone, Jude sat back and tried to assess his new company. "You're quite the force to be reckoned with."

"Thank you, I try. Now run the adopted thing by me again?"

"I would if I could get two thoughts to sit next to each other. So I'm obliterating all thoughts entirely. Or trying."

"I got a better means of obliterating thoughts. Without the debilitating hangover."

Again, the Jude that Jude knew, who hated this kind of come-on, was nowhere to be found. Tej was making him preen a little. Sit back in relaxed confidence and accept his due.

"What are you smiling about," Tej said.

"Normally, arrogant audacity turns me off. But I'm rather enjoying this pick-up."

"And this is my bare minimum effort. Can you imagine if I really turned on the charm?"

"I might combust."

"Hopefully."

As fast as the confident rush came, it left. Jude felt his face flame up as all clever comebacks deserted him. "I don't really have the wherewithal to spar with you right now."

"Do you have the wherewithal to fuck with me?"

"Dude... You can't say shit like that."

"Why not?"

Because it's giving me a hard-on. "Didn't your mother ever tell you not to talk to strangers?"

"Talking to strangers gets you laid."

"Jesus."

"Besides, we stopped being strangers five minutes ago. So let's stop talking and get out of here."

"Shut up."

Tej leaned his chin on the heel of his hand. "You're actually giving this some thought."

"What I'm thinking is you're insane."

And I'm kind of loving it.

"Come home with me," Tej said, unperturbed. "I'll make you feel better. You get a good night's sleep and things will look clearer in the morning. And if they don't, at least you got laid."

"I'm a lousy lay when I'm distracted."

"I'll have to work harder at holding your attention then."

Jude held still, knowing the slightest attempt to readjust the erection in his jeans would not only be detected, but remarked upon. "This is extremely flattering," he said. "But I don't go home with strangers."

Tej jerked his head toward the back of the pub. "We could go in the loo."

Jude lowered his laughing face into his hands. "Who

are you?"

The waitress returned with their drinks. "Here you go, fellows."

Tej tugged at the pocket of her apron. "Rosie, I need a favor."

"What, baby?"

"I'm attempting to seduce this gorgeous gentleman and he's wisely being prudent about consorting with arrogant and audacious men he doesn't know."

"In other words, Tuesday."

Tej pointed a finger. "That was unnecessary."

"Sorry. Where do I come into the seduction scheme?"

"You already know everything about me. Can I ask you to please note his description?"

Rosie looked at Jude and winked. "With pleasure."

"Perhaps he'll give you his contact information. And if he goes missing in the morning or is found floating in the harbor, you report me to the police with all due dispatch."

"You are the dispatch."

"This is true."

Her empty tray on her hip, Rosie smiled at Jude. "For real, he's an EMD. He answers nine-one-one calls."

"No shit," Jude said.

"I do know where he lives. And all his secrets. He talks a big game but he's really a mush. You could do worse."

"Hey, hey, hey," Tej said. "I don't recall asking for this."

Rosie ruffled his hair. "Good luck. Both of you."

Jude watched her walk off. "Your sister?"

"I wish. So what do you think?"

But the second the word *sister* slid through Jude's teeth, it free-associated into siblings, lost children, unknown family and *who am I?* And then for fuck's sake, he was tearing up. What, he was going to fucking cry about this? He never cried. Not anymore.

"Hey." Like a curtain falling, the teasing dropped out of Tej's face. In an instant he went from unknown libertine to trusted companion. "Hey, it's okay. I'm sorry. You're legit upset. I'll let you be."

Jude felt an odd stab of panic at the thought of this guy *leaving* him anywhere. "No, no," he said, shaking the episode off hard and getting what shit he had together. "It's just... I'm a sloppy drunk."

"You're not drooling or slurring."

"Yet."

"I'm bold but I'm not stupid. I can see whatever's going on, it's hurting like hell. I'm sorry."

"I typically try much harder than this to make a good first impression."

"There's something to be said for getting your worst moments over with."

Jude raised his glass. "Welcome to my shit show."

Tej clinked his against it. "I've seen worse."

"Yeah?"

"Yeah. Anyone ever tell you you look a little bit like Daniel Westling?"

"Who?"

"Daniel Westling. Prince consort of Sweden."

"No."

"Well, I'll be the first then." Tej held up his glass. "Skål."

They drank, eyes locked over the rims of their glasses. Beneath the table, the slightest, tiniest pressure: the toe of Tej's shoe against the toe of Jude's. It sent a tiny current up Jude's calf.

"Don't look at me like that," he heard himself say.

"Like what?"

Like you want to fuck me.

"Like...that."

Tej reached and pushed Jude's glass back down to the table. "Come on. You're cut off and so am I. This was fun, but now let's find you a cab."

They didn't do-si-do around the bill. Each put money on the table. Jude pulled on his jacket and Tej went to retrieve his from wherever he'd left it. Outside, the air was icy and bracing.

"I think I'll walk a little," Jude said, inhaling deep into his stomach.

"I'll come with."

"You will?"

"If you don't mind."

"Okay?"

Tej crossed his arms, eyes flicking to the skies. "Don't look so surprised. You're nineteen kinds of gorgeous, but you also look like your life's been turned inside-out. I feel bad."

"I'll be all right."

Tej took a step in. "Don't misunderstand me."

"Mm?"

"My only goal tonight is to get you safe in a cab home. But it doesn't mean I don't want to get you naked."

Jude filled with curious and arrogant heat. As the cold night enveloped him, he was shocked steam didn't start rising off his body. "I see."

"And not for nothing, but I want that pretty bad."

"You don't even know me."

"Instinctive lust. It serves a certain purpose."

Son of a bitch, the heat switched off and Jude was freezing cold. And light-headed all of a sudden. He put a hand against the building's brick façade. "Oh man, I'm wasted."

Tej touched his elbow. "You okay?"

"I swear, I don't..." He laughed softly as he drew in breath after breath. "This isn't me."

"No, I think it is you. And I'm digging it."

"Bullshit."

"No really. And whatever's hurting you, I want to make it stop." The fingertips on Jude's elbow turned into a palm, then a warm, strong grip around his bicep.

"Who *are* you?" Jude whispered, staring at Tej's mouth.

Tej's smile—quick, wide and true—was a beautiful thing. "I'm just me."

Jude stared, caught up in the moment that wanted him

to trust it so badly.

Tej leaned in a little. "It's me."

His other hand ran lightly through the hair above Jude's ear.

"Only me."

He closed the gap and rested his mouth against Jude's. Soft and neutral, letting Jude get used to his proximity. Jude closed his eyes and leaned into the kiss. Opened for it. Slid down it, falling through the darkness behind his eyelids.

"You taste amazing," Tej said against Jude's chin.

"So do you."

"Feel better?"

"Yeah. That was...rather head-clearing actually."

"You want to walk or find that cab?"

"Neither." He pulled Tej back in, turning them so Tej's shoulders were up against the bricks now. His fists full of Tej's jacket, he kissed him. Opening his mouth a little more, inviting the slide of tongue and the edge of teeth. Following it back into Tej's mouth, swallowing his breath, echoing back a sharp moan in his throat.

"Damn," Tej said, breathing hard. "I didn't think this would actually work."

"Now I know you're crazy."

Tej slid hands into Jude's back pockets. "Crazy also serves a certain purpose."

Jude planted his palms against the wall. Their eyes held a long moment, shoulders and chests rising and falling in unison. Breathing their way through a decision.

"Whatever you want to do," Tej said. "Nothing. Everything. Something. It's fine. I just want you to be all right."

"I think I just want you."

The Tiger

"You all right?"

"Oh I'm fine..."

She was fine and Roger had been fucking her from hell to breakfast with no end in sight. Whether there was true power in that powdered tree bark, or it was simply power of suggestion, it didn't matter: the tiger had found him. He could go on until dawn. Holding back took no effort at all. He felt amazing. Every one of his senses seemed to be heightened, yet at the same time there was the tiniest disassociation between mind and body. His sexuality was here, right here, intense and delicious and fully present. But his participation was ever so slightly separated, and that part was the tiger, calmly watching, overseeing, declaring *Not you yet. Her now. You later.*

He couldn't have cared less about later. The *now* of her now was endless. She was endless. He was rewound, seeing her as if for the first time. Everything about her was wonderful, everything was new and astonishing and there for the taking.

He took it slow. Out on their small, secluded veranda,

they'd danced for a long time, and he reveled in her kiss, in the way their mouths fit, the slide of her tongue and the little way she gently ran her teeth on his bottom lip. He took off her top, unhooked her bra and paid a lot of loving attention to her breasts—God, when was the last time he'd hung out on second for a good long while? He was lost in them, in their curves and weight and scent and her nipples hard in his mouth.

"I love this," Stav sighed, holding his head, her back arching into his touch.

Gradually they made their way back inside, to where the smooth expanse of the king-sized bed yawned before them, beckoning like a giant hand for them to fall into its palm. They left the doors to the outside open for there was nobody and nothing but the ocean to hear them. He slid her skirt off, laid her down and kissed her from crown to toes until she was spreading her legs and writhing, writhing, she could not hold still she wanted him so bad. He took his time, took a small eternity to get her panties down until she actually threatened to kill him.

Which was awesome.

Even with his life in jeopardy, he benignly ignored her small moans and impatient whimpers, his fingers gently peeling her open, looking at her, touching that pink, trembling flesh, satisfying this enhanced curiosity and making her wait until her fists were beating against the mattress and she was begging for his mouth, begging out loud, *Please, Rog, please lick me.*

Which was *awesome.*

When he worked his tongue gently into that heat, it quivered. She went wild on him. She twisted and bucked but he held her hips still and happily went down on her. She was crazed, but he was almost casual, practically humming with contentment, aware of every fold and crevice, every nuance of taste and texture, combining his mouth with his fingers until she came like a hurricane, her nails digging in his arms, her legs flailing wildly on his shoulders.

She rolled over and reached to pull him down on her back, but then the tiger went savage and this was just the start. He wasn't going to just make her come, folks, he was going to make her *scream*. He dragged her, literally dragged her by the legs to edge of the bed and there he bent her over, held her down, stood over her and proceeded to fuck her senseless. It was torrid. It was magnificent. She was a glorious wreck under him, off in some filthy, primal place he had never seen her go before, verbally raw and lavish in her praise of him. He was her man. She loved his cock in her. Nobody fucked her like him. He was good. He was so good. He fucked her so good. He was going to make her come. She was going to come again.

He knew. He could feel it building in her, feel her squeeze and pulse around him, feel her lengthen and expand so that he was moving further and further into her with each thrust. He could feel it and he could hear it, too. Her face was crushed in a pillow, but tonight Stav was making some serious noise. Roger had her hands pulled up tight in the small of her back and he was loving like a tiger and she was his prey and now it was on her. He was getting her off and *yes*, she was screaming now. And normally that would ricochet back and knock him over the edge as well, but tonight, he simply watched her, watched it from beginning to end, with a fascinated mix of pleasure and pride.

Slowly, the storm passed, her body quieted. He gently let go of her wrists and caressed the long curves of her sides, let her rest, catch her breath and demand of him, with no small degree of awe, "What is with you tonight?"

He smoothed her hair back from her flushed face, and his heart contracted. This was the love of his life, his treasure. The tiger turned again, tame and tender now. He rolled her over to face him, slid one arm under the small of her back, the other under her shoulders and moved her further up the mattress. He stretched out full on top of her, cradled in her thighs, settled into her and moved there with a relaxed languor. Infinitely patient as he kissed her, her head held fast in his hands.

"You're so good," she whispered. "You're so, so good."

Time stretched out into meaningless lengths. They stared. They kissed. He moved in her, ran his thumb over her swollen mouth, kissed that mouth opened and closed. He whispered things to make her smile, just so he could feel the shape of her face change against his palm. He whispered things to make her sigh, just so he could feel the vibration against his chest. "I love you so much," he said, softly desperate.

"I love you," she whispered, gazing up at him, her arms around his neck, fingers sliding through his hair.

"Let's just make love forever."

"Fuck everything."

"Everything," he agreed. "Tell me what you want. I'll do anything you want."

She kissed him a long, slow time, then whispered, "I want to feel your tongue again."

He slid out of her and inched backward, brought her knees together, pushed them up to her chest, lay his forearm against the back of her thighs and licked her again. Slowly, gently, running his thumb along that slick pinkness and following with his tongue and her voice floated over him, moaning his name, calling to him in the dark. Not wild now, just quietly ecstatic. When she came this time it was not as a leap into destruction, but an effortless fall into safety. Then he sat back on his knees, picked her hips up and into his lap, and slid into her again.

It went on for hours, the tiger shaping the mood of their lovemaking, shifting and morphing, turning and twisting. He touched her, licked her, tasted her, loved her, fucked her from every side and every angle until she was utterly spent and sated, unable to make any more noise or even form his name. Then and only then did the great cat acquiesce and agree to join the rest of his body again.

Now you.

"My God," she murmured against his mouth, reaching down and closing him up in her hands. "You have the best cock."

He laughed and pushed his face into her neck. He was still rock hard and raring but now completely connected to the moment. Suddenly vulnerable. Almost shy. He lay on his side, stretched out full, the tiger having done his tricks now getting his treats. She lay alongside him, her forehead against his lower belly and gathered him into her mouth. His hand lovingly moved in the damp hair at the back of her head. His thumb lightly traced her mouth, feeling how her lips were shaped around him, the flex of her jaw as she took him down deep. He shut his eyes, curled his toes and let all that wonderful, warm, wet heat engulf him.

Soon she gentled him down on his back, climbed on top and lowered her hips down, pulling him inside her. At the sight of her looming over him, desire-laced adrenaline smacked him full in the chest and began coursing through his limbs. He was undone, dire and desperate, pulling her down, pulling her mouth into his. He wanted to drink her, swallow her, his cock was aching and he couldn't get it deep enough into her body. She couldn't be enough his. She was a tigress, giving him back everything he'd given her, fucking him fast and hard, then slithering away and going down on him. Bringing him to the brink, then getting up on him again, facing his legs this time, shaking her hair down her back. She leaned on his shins, gave him the view of her, gave him her best, gave him everything. And when it came crashing down on him, he clutched her hips and roared into the night and put it all into her.

Later, whispered pillow talk in the dark.

"That was crazy...What did he call that stuff?"

"Bois bandé."

A long pause. He was nodding off in the circle of her arms, the edges of his mind unraveling. Her breathing was soft and slow. Then suddenly she gave a start and swatted his shoulder. "Bois bandé."

"Speaking," he said sleepily.

"Bois is French for wood."

He chuckled. It certainly was.

"And bandé," she said. "Bander means to have an erection. Duh. Of course."

They lay laughing and whispering, slowly drifting off in the big bed, arms and legs tangled like vines as the curtains danced in the beach breeze.

"Stav?"

"Hm?"

"It's still hard."

Her hands caressed his back. "Go to sleep."

Stories About the Stories

Blind: I wrote this in the early nineties when I was working at MCI in New York City. I was invited to a team lunch at Carmine's on 45th Street. The food was phenomenal and I'd never eaten in a family-style restaurant before. Dressed in my dress suit and heels, laughing and feasting with my co-workers, passing dishes up and down the table, I felt very hip and grown-up. And garlicky, wow. Dragon breath for days after, but so worth it.

Incidentally, my parents met on a blind date. They've now been married 56 years. True story.

Your Name: Another scribble from the early nineties as I relocated one of my many tragic heroes from the US to Canada. I honestly don't remember why I picked Saint John, New Brunswick as a setting, but it went on to feature prominently in my *Fish Tales* series. Anyway, when I was commuting by train in the city, there was this woman I saw all the time. She was always so beautiful and put-together. I admired her clothes and shoes and how she wore her hair. And I developed this small voyeuristic crush as I tried to guess her name. I never did find out. I don't think I wanted to.

Short For?: This scene used to be a girl-meets-boy vignette and Sam was Nina. (Nina from "Blind." I know. It's confusing.) It was cute but it always seemed a little "meh" to me. Like it had all been done before. Same old, same old. I tried a name change, which sometimes works, and made Nina into Samantha. Which of course got shortened to Sam and... Wait... Sam. Sam? Is Sam a guy? I started changing some "shes" to "hes" and shazam, it was suddenly a whole different story. I love when that happens.

Talking to Strangers: This is an excerpt from my novel *A Scarcity of Condors*. It was the first thing I wrote. I had no choice: Tej Khoury bashed out of my head and onto the page, telling me exactly who he was and what he wanted and no, he didn't need any revisions, thank you very much. I said "challenge accepted" and this scene went verbatim into the novel.

Most of the other stories came from being in a writing group. We had a challenge of "I'll give a country, you give me a sex scene." The goal was to take the time, do the homework and make the location a third party in the scene. Then we'd vote on a winner.

The group leader started out nice to us: Paris, Saint Lucia, Bali. Places conducive to romance. Then it got a little more challenging. Antarctica, for instance. Lots of layers of clothing to negotiate, constant daylight to draw the drapes against. By the way, did you know that Rothera Research Station on Adelaide Island has a house band? The band is called Nunatek. Go forth to parties and impress people. You're welcome.

Thank You

WHAT DOES AN AUTHOR stand to gain by giving away a free book? A lot. In fact, what we can gain is so important in the publishing world, that they've coined a catchy name for it.

It's called "social proof."

And in this age of social media sharing, without social proof, an author may as well be invisible.

So if you've enjoyed Love & Bravery, please consider giving it some visibility by reviewing it on Amazon or Goodreads. A review doesn't have to be a long critical essay. Just a few words expressing your thoughts, which could help potential readers decide whether they would enjoy these little stories too.

Wishing you love and bravery in all your journeys on earth.

Fazendo tudo.

ABOUT THE AUTHOR

A FORMER PROFESSIONAL DANCER and teacher, Suanne Laqueur went from choreographing music to choreographing words. Her work has been described as therapy fiction, emotionally intelligent romance and contemporary train wreck.

Laqueur's novel *An Exaltation of Larks* was the Grand Prize winner in the 2017 Writer's Digest Awards and won first place in the 2019 North Street Book Prize. Her debut novel *The Man I Love* won a gold medal in the 2015 Readers' Favorite Book Awards and was named Best Debut in the Feathered Quill Book Awards. Her follow-up novel, *Give Me Your Answer True*, was also a gold medal winner at the 2016 RFBA.

Laqueur graduated from Alfred University with a double major in dance and theater. She taught at the Carol Bierman School of Ballet Arts in Croton-on-Hudson for ten years. An avid reader, cook and gardener, she started her blog EatsReadsThinks in 2010.

Suanne lives in Westchester County, New York with her husband and two children.

Visit her at suannelaqueurwrites.com

All feels welcome. And she always has coffee.

ALSO BY SUANNE LAQUEUR

THE FISH TALES

The Man I Love
Give Me Your Answer True
Here to Stay
The Ones That Got Away

VENERY

An Exaltation of Larks
A Charm of Finches
A Scarcity of Condors
The Voyages of Trueblood Cay
Tales from Cushman Row
A Plump of Woodcocks

SHORT STORIES

Love & Bravery
An Evening at the Hotel

GIVEAWAY

Enter to win a signed copy of An Exaltation of Larks
All entrants receive a free ebook of The Man I Love
http://lqrwrites.com/freebook